COWBOY BODYGUARD

Cowboy Confidential Book 4

LORI WILDE &

KRISTIN ECKHARDT

I

Something was out there.

Jack Holden stilled in the saddle and tugged gently on the reins to slow his horse, Scout, to a stop. The bay gelding obeyed immediately, not making a sound. He'd trained the quarter horse himself and reached down to gently pat its neck.

Then his gaze scanned the fence line, overgrown with brush and shadowed by the thick grove of trees surrounding it. Only a sliver of moonlight shone in the dark Texas sky and tree branches swayed in the warm August breeze. An owl hooted in the distance as Jack slowly dismounted to assess his surroundings.

Static suddenly crackled in his earpiece, then a voice said, "Possible breach near the east fence. Holden, that's your zone."

"I'm on it," Jack replied, keeping his voice low.

After his honorable discharge from the Army eight years ago, he'd taken a job with Tuf Security in Pine City. It was a private firm that provided bodyguards and event security for high-profile business executives, professional athletes, entertainers, or anyone who might be a target due to their wealth or fame. Tonight, they were working a party at the ritzy Cumberland Ranch, where all the bigwigs in North Texas had gathered for a charity ball.

Leaving Scout to graze on the lush grass, he began to walk along the high fence constructed of thick wood beams and steel. It wouldn't be easy to breach, but someone determined enough to climb over it could gain entrance. He made a mental note to advise the Cumberlands to upgrade their fence security.

After several minutes of walking along the east fence, he'd almost convinced himself that the breach was a false alarm. Probably just some critter making too much noise, he thought to himself, like a deer or a coyote. As his gaze surveyed the area once more, he just hoped it wasn't a skunk.

Then he noticed a figure in the distance, emerging from beneath the long shadow of tree branches. It was too dark and far away for him to make out more than a silhouette, but there was *definitely* someone out there.

Maybe a two-legged skunk.

Jack pressed one finger to his earpiece and said softly, "Intruder sighted."

"Need backup?"

He sized up the lone subject, then replied. "Nah, I've got this."

Then he advanced, moving quickly toward his target. "Stop right there," he commanded, reaching for the gun in his shoulder harness. "Put your hands up and identify yourself!"

"Don't you dare shoot me, Jack Beauregard Holden," cried a voice he knew all too well. "You've been avoiding me for so long I finally had to track you down myself!"

Jack lowered his gun, shock and disbelief reverberating through him. "Grandma Hattie?"

"For land's sake, put that gun away, boy." Grandma Hattie, dressed all in black, marched up to him. Then her expression softened. "I'm sorry if I gave you a start."

"A start?" he echoed, tipping up his cowboy hat. "What are you even doing here?"

"I had some business at the Cumberland house and decided to stop by to see you." Her silver brow furrowed, then she moved close enough to place her palm on his forehead. "You're looking a little pale. Do you feel all right?"

"I'm fine, Grandma," he assured her,

wondering how he'd ever explain pulling a gun on Grandma Hattie to his five brothers. She and their late grandfather had raised all six of them on Elk Creek Ranch after their parents were killed in a car accident. The Holden Brothers hadn't had a good brawl for a while, but he probably had one coming now. "What business did you have here?"

She dropped her hand from his forehead and patted his shoulder. "Oh, just some Cowboy Confidential business."

He swallowed a groan. Cowboy Confidential was Grandma Hattie's staffing company that she'd recently started out of her home on Elk Creek Ranch. She employed family members and friends to work temporary jobs for ranchers and farmers.

Although a few Cowboy Confidential jobs required a different kind of expertise. She'd been after Jack to take on one of those jobs in his spare time, but he'd been putting her off. Now he wondered what she had up her sleeve.

Before he could ask her, the voice sounded in his earpiece again. "Hey, Holden, do you have a status report?"

"The situation is under control," Jack replied. "I have the intruder secured and will follow protocol."

"Roger that," said the voice in his ear.

Then Jack turned to his grandmother and offered her his arm. "May I escort you back to the house?"

She smiled up at him as she smoothed back her silver hair. "I assume that's protocol?"

He nodded. "I need to take you to the command center for processing, but it's just a formality."

"Perfect," she replied, taking his arm. "That will give us plenty of time to catch up."

Fifteen minutes later, they arrived at the Cumberland mansion. Jack could hear loud band music emanating from the ballroom as he led his grandmother to the back of the house, where the housekeeper's small office served as a temporary command center for Tuf Security.

When they reached the open doorway to the office, Jack saw his old friend and owner of Tuf Security, Trevor Fleming, seated behind a small desk and talking on his cell phone.

Trevor smiled and waved them inside.

Jack pulled up a chair for Grandma Hattie and helped her sit down. But as he started to grab a chair for himself, he saw something that made his stomach drop. On the table behind Trevor there were six bottles of Grandma Hattie's homemade blackberry cordial. His gut told him he was being set up and the serene smile on Grandma Hattie's face sent him hurrying toward the door.

"Hold on there, Jack," Trevor called out.

Jack slowly turned around. "I need to get back to my post."

"This should only take a minute," Trevor said, pocketing his phone as he flashed a smile at Grandma Hattie. "I didn't expect to see you back here so soon, Hattie. Don't tell me you're the one who breached the fence?"

"I sure am," she replied. "I've been climbing fences since I was four years old. And I was bound and determined to see my grandson since you've been keeping him so busy."

Trevor nodded. "He's one of the best." Then he looked up at Jack. "In fact, a new job just landed on my desk and I think you're the perfect fit."

"Let me guess," Jack said with a sigh. "Is it a job with Cowboy Confidential?"

Trevor laughed. "How'd you know?"

"Like you said, I'm one of the best. Plus, I know you've always been a sucker for Grandma Hattie's blackberry cordial. And she only hands it out to Cowboy Confidential clients." Then he pointed to the six bottles of cordial. "But I've never seen her give out that many before."

Grandma Hattie sniffed. "It seems like a fair trade for Trevor lending me Tuf Security's best bodyguard."

"I agree," Trevor said.

Jack chuckled. His grandmother had finally done it. After months of Jack explaining to her that he was too busy to work for Cowboy Confidential, she'd found a way to rope him in. "Okay, I'm in. What's the job?"

Trevor grinned as he reached for a file on his desk and handed it over to Jack. "Protecting a damsel in distress. So, it's right up your alley."

Carly Weiss knew she'd never look at a cream puff the same way again. Especially now that her flaky pastry was Exhibit A in the case of the People versus Chester Frey.

It all began when she'd been hired by bookshop owner Sophie Odell to prepare a gourmet meal on the sly in Sophie's kitchen. Poor Sophie had been an ardent believer in the old adage that the quickest way to a man's heart is through his stomach. So, wanting to impress her new beau Tobias Cobb with her cooking, she'd had Carly hidden away in the kitchen, cooking her heart out, and handing the gourmet results to Sophie who had passed them off as her own.

Everything had been working out perfectly until Sophie's ex-boyfriend, Professor Chester Frey, showed up with a .357 magnum and gunned down Sophie and Tobias. The bullet that had blasted through Cobb, a sofa cushion, and an Oriental screen had finally turned up on a dessert plate, smothered in hazelnut cream filling.

Carly tried not to think of the shooting as a bad omen for her fledgling catering business. In fact, she tried not to think of the shooting at all. Or the blood. Or the chilling, calculated expression on Professor Frey's bearded face that had been haunting her sleep ever since.

It affected her so much that she even briefly considered her mother's pleas to marry and make babies instead of baklava. Fortunately, the shock gradually had faded, and Carly once again set her sights on her dream. She wanted to sauté her way to the top of the catering world. Or at least be the best in Pine City. Maybe even someday open her own gourmet restaurant.

Omens be damned. Her cooking hadn't actually killed anyone yet, even if she had witnessed two murders in the line of duty.

A savvy businesswoman couldn't allow one little mishap to deter her. However, a savvy businesswoman could take advantage of this opportunity. Especially an insolvent savvy businesswoman.

"My card," Carly said, handing Monica Cortez,

Pine City's seasoned district attorney, a small rectangular white parchment with the words Carly's Creations printed in big, bold letters, a stalk of asparagus serving as a colorful exclamation point. Then she sat down in a leather wing chair and watched an expression of blatant disbelief cross the woman's face as she stared at the business card. All right. So, it was shameless self-promotion. Some might even call it tacky.

Carly called it survival.

After the news of the shooting hit the media, most of her catering clients had decided murder wasn't all that appetizing. Soon her cell phone had been flooded with messages of condolence and cancellations.

Then the bank had started sending her loan notices with the word *overdue* printed in reproving red ink. Her suppliers kept hounding her for payment. And this morning her cheese soufflé had collapsed. A girl can only take so much pressure before she breaks.

Carly had succumbed to that pressure by donning her best power suit and wedging her feet into a pair of spiked Italian heels recommended by her Dress-For-Success class. Then she'd teetered down to the district attorney's office, ready to ask for a small favor. Prosecutors were always offering deals in exchange for testimony, weren't they? She watched reruns of *Law & Order*. She knew how the system worked.

"I'm so glad you're here, Ms. Weiss," Monica said. She opened a thick file folder on her desk and placed Carly's business card inside. "My office has been trying to reach you."

"Please call me Carly," she said, relaxing under Monica's affable smile. This wasn't so hard after all. Monica looked like a woman ready to bargain. "If it's about my testimony..."

The door creaked open behind her, and Carly turned and saw a cowboy framed in the doorway, his broad shoulders almost touching the casing. He was tall, even taller than her brothers, which made him at least six three, and all of it lean, hard muscle. When he took off his black cowboy hat, she noticed his close-cropped, black hair matched the dark shadow of stubble on his solid, square jaw. The cowboy boots, blue denim jeans, and black shirt he wore clashed with the opulent furnishings and soft, pastel colors of the office.

Carly reached up to adjust her glasses and realized after poking her finger into the bridge of her nose that she wasn't wearing them. That was the problem with nervous habits; they didn't adjust well to fashion concessions like contact lenses. Her cheeks grew warm as she dropped her hand back into her lap.

"Did Frey see you that night?" The deep baritone of his voice surprised her. And the way he walked into the room made it clear this cowboy thought he was in charge.

Carly swallowed her discomposure and her gum. "Who are you?"

"Jack Holden," he replied shortly, seating himself in a chair next to the window. He flipped open the clasp of the knapsack he held and withdrew a manila folder. He studied the contents for a moment, and then he studied Carly. "I understand you were hiding in Ms. Odell's kitchen."

"I wasn't actually *hiding* in the kitchen; I was just tucked away in there," she clarified. "Although after the shooting started, I was definitely cowering under the counter."

"Did you hear Professor Frey arrive?"

Carly bristled a little at how this handsome stranger had sauntered into the district attorney's office and started interrogating her without so much as a polite introduction. She wanted to put him in his place with a stinging rebuke. But the only word that came to mind when she looked at Jack Holden was *hunk-a-burger,* a nickname coined by Carly and her best friend Alma Jones in their adolescence to describe a mouthwatering male.

Lucky Alma satisfied her craving a year ago by marrying her very own hunk-a-burger named Stanley. Unfortunately, at twenty-nine, Carly's no-sizzle love life left her with plenty of time on her hands. So she poured all her passion into her work, creating such delectable dishes as wild plum pudding with hard sauce and steamy scallops on a bed of wild rice. Cooking provided a wonderful alternative to brooding about her solitary state.

Until she came face-to-face with temptation.

She met his intrepid gaze and said coolly, "Sophie cranked jazz music on her stereo so her date wouldn't hear me in the kitchen. She wanted him to believe *she* was doing all the cooking."

Poor, poor Sophie. Desperate for love and marriage, she'd sorted through her admirers, stamped Tobias Cobb as the brightest romantic prospect, and dumped Chester Frey like a moldy old book. No matter how this meeting turned out, Carly had every intention of testifying against Frey to make him pay for what he'd done to Sophie and Tobias.

"I stayed in the kitchen, braising and basting, the entire evening," Carly continued. "Sophie would come in there, spend a few minutes reading texts on her phone, and then walk out with the next gourmet course on a bamboo tray. I didn't hear anything but 'La Bamba' until the shooting started."

Jack Holden arched a black brow. "Braising and basting?"

"The duckling a l'orange. It's a touchy dish," Carly explained. "Cook it too long and it's dry, not long enough and it's tough." Reaching into her purse, she pulled out another business card and handed it to him. "I'd love to make it for you sometime."

Startled, Jack took the card, realizing he never met anyone who mixed business with murder before. But then everything about this witness was unique. From her thick mane of unruly chestnut curls to her deep indigo-blue eyes to her provocative mouth. Even the small beauty mark on her left cheek. He tried to ignore how well she filled out her black-and-white pantsuit, cinched at her narrow waist with a wide black belt that only accentuated the feminine curves both atop and below it. Jack cleared his throat and looked away, reminding himself that he had rules about this sort of thing.

"You never answered my question," he told her as he pocketed the card and focused his attention back where it belonged. "Did the professor see you that night?"

"Of course not," Carly replied. "I only cracked open the shutters that separated the kitchen from the rest of the apartment when I heard the gun blast. That's when I saw him shoot up everything in that room, including Sophie's collection of stuffed teddy bears. I don't think he would've spared me, even if I do make the world's best meatloaf."

"Believe it or not, Jack hates meatloaf," Monica said. "How would you like the opportunity to convert him?"

The perfect opening. Carly seized it with both oven mitts. "I'd love to cater a meal for Mr. Holden. For both of you, actually. I understand you're up for reelection, Ms. Boyle," she said, sitting forward in her chair, her voice full of enthusiasm. "Carly's Creations can provide the perfect menu to open up those campaign pocketbooks. How does oysters in champagne sauce sound? Then we could follow with celery consommé and a light entree. Perhaps lamb curry or Veal Normande? The dessert should be both elegant and powerful." She paused a moment, her gaze assessing the older woman. "Chocolate crepes with French vanilla sauce, I think."

"It all sounds delightful." Monica Boyle folded her hands on top of her desk, her polished fingernails a perfect match to her Chanel suit. "But I'm talking about placing you under Jack's protection. Just as a simple precaution, of course, until the trial."

"Wait a minute, he's a *bodyguard?*" Carly interjected, the word sticking in her throat. "Isn't that a little extreme? I mean, Chester Frey is behind bars."

"That seems to be the problem," Jack said. He shuffled through the papers in his folder, finally pulling out a single sheet of lavender stationery. He studied it for a moment, his brow furrowed, then handed it to her. "This came to our attention this morning."

The drawing on the crinkled paper drew her notice first. It was a small caricature of a woman's face, done in crayon, with huge blue eyes and bushy, brown hair. Below the picture were four short lines of verse, also in crayon. The letters were written in an indistinguishable block print.

SUGAR, SPICE, AND EVERYTHING NICE, GO INTO COOKIES AND CAKE. FALSEHOODS, FIBS AND OUTRIGHT LIES DO A DEAD CATERER MAKE.

"This is awful," Carly breathed. "*Lies* doesn't rhyme with *nice.* And what's this supposed to be?" She pointed to the drawing. "A witch?"

Jack folded his arms across his chest, his

gunmetal-gray eyes unreadable. "That is a picture of you, Ms. Weiss."

Carly's mouth dropped open in horror as she studied the picture again. He was right. The coloring matched. Even the small dark spot on her cheek. She looked up at him in dismay. "Is my nose really that big?"

"No," Jack replied crisply. He took the paper out of her hands and returned it to the folder. "But I think you're missing the point. This may indicate a threat to your life."

Carly smiled. "From whom? A vengeful preschooler?" She sobered when she saw a muscle begin to twitch in Jack's jaw. The man obviously had no sense of humor.

"This is serious," he replied. "Frey claims he received this letter in his mail yesterday at the jailhouse. I'm sure you know that he's somewhat of a minor celebrity?"

"He wrote The Top Ten Traits of True Love," Carly said.

Jack nodded. "This letter may have come from a deranged fan who doesn't want to see his idol spend the rest of his life in prison. Now I don't want to alarm you..."

"Of course not," Monica interrupted. "That is certainly not our intention." She stood up and walked around to the front of her desk. "We hope the note is nothing more than a hoax. But our department does have certain guidelines we follow in this type of situation." Her voice grew wistful. "Professor Frey is... was... highly admired in academic circles. His seminars were quite popular, as well as his books. I believe *Loving Your Neighbor* even appeared briefly on the bestseller list." She smiled reassuringly at Carly. "It's not unusual for celebrities to receive correspondence such as this. Most of the time it comes to nothing."

Jack watched Monica at work and wondered when and where she learned to spin so beautifully. He supposed it was a natural result of a lifetime in public office. But now that distinguished career was in jeopardy. He'd met with her yesterday and learned about the case. Recent newspaper editorials were questioning the district attorney's commitment to this case since she and Frey belonged to the same Pine City social circle. As members of an exclusive country club, they both frequently attended the same parties and formal dinners.

He'd also learned that his brother Nick, a police detective involved in the case, was the one who referred Monica to Cowboy Confidential for bodyguard services.

Jack cleared his throat. "I believe the professor also fits the classic portrait of a sociopath. A man who believes himself intellectually superior to others. It's not inconceivable that he's manufactured this so-called anonymous letter just to unnerve you, Ms. Weiss. Like a puppet master pulling strings. It's an issue of power. He knows the D.A.'s office can't just ignore something like this."

Monica frowned at him. "It's possible. Although I believe Professor Frey gave us this letter in good faith. He claims he has no wish to see another human being harmed."

Carly gaped at her in astonishment. "Is this the same man who sent the love of his life and her date on a one-way trip to the Woodlawn Cemetery?"

Jack observed Monica's cheeks darken. The lady didn't like dissenters. But Carly Weiss, the only witness in an otherwise shaky circumstantial evidence case, was the key to getting Frey convicted. The man was still professing his innocence and was charming and articulate enough to potentially convince a jury of it, too. *If* Carly wasn't there to contradict him.

Most people believed Monica's reelection hinged on his conviction. She needed to portray herself as a tough prosecutor—which meant keeping her best witness alive and well and happy.

"You're so right," Monica acquiesced. "Now you know why we're concerned about your safety. Jack is one of the best bodyguards in the business. And due to a special witness protection fund, we're able to offer his services to you. I'm certain he'll strive to inconvenience your life as little as possible."

"Thank you," Carly said politely, "but no thank you."

Monica's brown eyes widened behind her bifocals. "I beg your pardon?"

Carly smiled apologetically at Jack. "I really don't think I need a bodyguard. I appreciate your concern, but I'm perfectly capable of taking care of myself. The trial is only two weeks away and..."

"Four," Jack interjected. "Frey got a postponement."

Carly shifted in her chair. At this precise moment, Jack Holden was disturbing her far more than some lousy poem. Tiny goose bumps rose on her neck as his intense gray eyes regarded her. His firm, oddly sensual mouth was set in a determined line.

"Ms. Weiss, I must insist that you consider this very carefully," Monica Boyle said. "It's just a precaution, of course, but a necessary one."

Glimpsing an employment opportunity, Carly instantly set her misgivings about Jack aside. "I disagree," she began. "Since the murder, my business has suffered terribly." She sighed dramatically. "I'll probably just spend the next four weeks holed up in my apartment, developing new, tantalizing recipes. Unless you happen to know someone who could use my catering services."

Monica Boyle's blond brow rose a fraction. "I might."

Carly smiled dolefully at her, hoping she looked the picture of the noble but suffering capitalist—hoping her bluff worked for the sake of Carly's Creations' financial statement.

D.A. Boyle returned the smile, though her eyes remained cool. "Perhaps you'd consider catering a campaign kickoff luncheon I'm planning?" She paused a beat. "Of course, I wouldn't consider hiring you unless Jack was also present as your full-time bodyguard. For the safety of both you and my guests."

Carly pretended to consider the offer. "I suppose that's reasonable, since there will probably be several high-level city officials invited. Maybe a few city councilmen, a judge or two..."

"Even the mayor," Monica said dryly. "Do we have a deal?"

"We need to set some ground rules," Jack announced as he followed Carly through the door of her apartment building. He carried his overnight bag in one hand and a sack of hastily packed groceries from his place in the other. The moment he stepped over the threshold, he realized the bunkhouse at Elk Creek Ranch would be more secure than this place.

"I don't like rules," Carly said, leading him down the dim hallway. A lone, willowy cobweb hung from the naked lightbulb in the ceiling. "But I suppose since this is an unusual situation, I can make an exception."

Force of habit made him check out every window and doorway, but his gaze kept being drawn back to the hypnotic sway of her rounded hips. Maybe this assignment was some sort of test. Like a stress test or one designed to measure how long he could withstand torture.

If he didn't know better, he'd think Grandma Hattie and Nick had conspired to find a woman with just the right combination of beauty, brains, and brass to make him want to kill her or kiss before he completed this job.

Jack loosened his grip on the leather handle of his overnight bag. Fortunately he had no intention of succumbing to either temptation.

Growing up on Elk Creek Ranch with five rowdy brothers had taught him to be tough, both inside and out. And losing his parents when he was only six years old had driven him to a career of protecting people so their families wouldn't have to live with that kind of pain and grief. That had always been his mission, and no one had distracted him from it —until now.

The floor squeaked as they made the long trek to the elevator. Grimy fingerprints smudged the puce-green walls and the distinct odor of overcooked cabbage wafted through the hallway.

Home for the next four weeks.

Jack smiled grimly to himself. At least now she was cooperating. Not a murmur of discontent passed her lips since they left the district attorney's office. Maybe this Cowboy Confidential job wouldn't be so difficult after all. Now that she got what she wanted, Carly Weiss, caterer and con artist extraordinaire, might not object to following orders.

"The first rule is no smoking or vaping," Carly began, stabbing the elevator button with one finger. "The odor can be absorbed into food and alter the taste."

The sickly ding of the elevator heralded its arrival. They waited several silent moments before the doors finally opened. Then they stepped into the empty car and Carly punched the number three button with her fist. She waited a few seconds, then punched it again. The doors closed with a groan as the elevator lurched upward.

"Nice place," Jack said, looking around the elevator car for an inspection sticker.

"It's not so bad," Carly replied, "once you know how everything works." She turned to face him, poked her finger into the bridge of her nose, and then clasped her hands behind her back. "Now what were we talking about...? Oh, yes, the ground rules."

She smiled up at him and Jack's stomach flipped over. A typical reaction in an elevator, he told himself firmly. Especially a rickety old crate like this one.

"The second rule is no running, jumping, or tumbling in the apartment," Carly informed him. "Mrs. Kolinski from downstairs retaliates by flushing her toilet whenever I'm in the shower."

"I'll try to restrain myself."

"Rule three is that we tell everyone you're my first cousin on my mother's side, visiting from Fort Worth for a few weeks before you make your annual trek to Anchorage, Alaska, to train for the Iditarod dogsled race. You keep your pack of champion malamutes in a kennel up there and pay a local kid to feed and care for them."

He bit back a smile. "As long as we keep it simple."

"Hey, if we have to put up with each other, we might as well make it interesting."

The elevator dinged, then lurched to a stop, but

the doors stayed firmly closed. Jack reached over and pushed the button.

Nothing happened.

“Here's the thing,” Carly said, her hands on her hips, “I really don’t care what most people think. That I picked you up at some honky-tonk or that we’re sleeping together...” Her gaze dropped from his face to his chest and her cheeks flushed a becoming petal pink. “Or even the truth—that you’re guarding me from a mad pen pal. I just don’t want Rusty from across the hall to get the wrong idea.”

“Rusty?” Jack echoed. He didn’t like the way she said his name. All soft and sweet. As if a guy with a name like Rusty deserved a woman like her.

Carly sighed. “He’s asked me out four times in the last year and I’ve always turned him down. Which is difficult because he’s very sensitive. If he thinks you and I are living together, his feelings might be hurt.”

Jack nodded, his dislike for Rusty now replaced by pity for the poor, rejected sap. “So, when I run into Rusty, I’m your cousin, the dogsled driver?”

“Right.” Her lips parted in a relieved smile, revealing a row of even, white teeth. "He'll like that."

Jack liked her smile. It even seemed to brighten up the dingy elevator. “How will I recognize him?”

“He’s shorter than you, always wears a baseball cap, and he has no eyebrows. He’s also very nice and lets me use his Wi-Fi password, because I can't afford internet at the moment."

Remembering her antics in the district attorney's office, he asked, "Just how did you finagle that?"

"I make spaetzle for him twice a month. It's his favorite."

Carly turned and smacked the center of the closed elevator doors with her fist. She waited a few seconds, then hit them again. The elevator doors finally creaked slowly open.

"Ever think about taking the stairs?" he asked, stepping warily out onto firmer ground. The sixth floor of the Sagebrush Apartments wasn't any more impressive than the first. Slim black cables dangled like snakes out of a hole in the ceiling. A poorly painted picture of rodeo clowns hung crookedly on the wall.

Carly shook her head, her thick chestnut curls bouncing against her back and shoulders. "The elevator's perfectly safe. Just some kind of wiring problem. I got stuck in there one afternoon for two hours," she explained, "and figured out how to work it." She looked up at him, her indigo eyes glowing with pride. "Just punch the doors right at the seam, count to five, and then punch them again. Works like a charm."

She turned, straightened the crooked picture, and started down the hallway. "Oh, I almost forgot."

Carly pivoted on her heel and stopped in front of him. "Rule four."

He shifted the grocery bag into the crook of his arm. "I can't wait to hear it."

Carly folded her arms across her chest. "I don't want you to touch my breasts."

Jack stepped back a pace. "I—I won't," he sputtered. "I haven't even considered it." All right. So he'd looked at them once, maybe six times. He wasn't obsessive about it, and he certainly didn't mean to offend her.

"Well, of course you haven't yet," Carly said, a flicker of amusement curving her lips. "I mean when we get into the apartment."

What exactly did she have in mind for the next four weeks? He concentrated on keeping his gaze fixed on her face. "Look, Carly. I'm here to protect you. That's all. I have a firm rule against becoming romantically involved with women under my protection." Jack took a deep breath and tried to let her down easy. "It's nothing personal. You're an attractive, appealing woman. Perhaps under different circumstances..."

"I'm talking about my pheasant breasts," she cut in, her cheeks turning red. "They're setting up in the refrigerator. The Chaud-Froid sauce is very delicate. I want to make sure it adheres perfectly to the meat."

Of course. The Chaud-Froid sauce. He should have guessed.

"Watch out for the pumpkin mousse, too. If it gets pushed to the back of the fridge it might freeze." She frowned at the bulging grocery bag in his arm. "In fact, maybe I better just clear a refrigerator shelf for you. Then we can avoid any problems."

Jack licked the sweat off his upper lip. "I won't touch anything of yours," he vowed. "Is that all?"

Carly nodded. "For now."

"Good." He needed to get control of this situation. Before she finessed him into getting what she wanted... like she did with the district attorney... and Rusty. "Then it's my turn. Rule number one..." he began sternly.

"Wait a minute," she interrupted. "You can't have rules. The D.A. promised me you'd inconvenience me as little as possible. That I'd hardly notice you. How is that possible when I'm forced to follow some endless list of rules?"

"How about if we just start off with one rule?"

Carly scowled. "That's still one too many. I moved three hundred miles away from home so I wouldn't have to follow rules anymore. Besides," she said, striding down the hallway, "it's my apartment. You can't tell me what to do."

"Rule number one," he said, easily keeping pace with her, "is that you do exactly as I tell you."

He couldn't help but smile at her exclamation of disbelief.

"No wonder you only need one rule! Of all the ridiculous, autocratic, controlling..." She stopped in front of a battered door and dug in her voluminous purse for her keys.

"Don't you have a dead bolt?" he asked, frowning at her flimsy doorknob. It looked about as sturdy as the rest of the building.

"Of course," she retorted. "My brother Robby gave me one last year for Christmas." She tipped her purse out onto the grungy, frayed red carpet and sifted through the debris. "I just haven't had time to put it in yet. Aha!" Carly held up her key ring in triumph.

Jack took the key from her and inserted it into the lock. "You stay right here until I check out the apartment."

"No, thank you," she replied, shoveling the contents of her purse back into the bag.

"This matter isn't open for negotiation. If you don't..."

They both froze at the sound of shattering glass emanating from somewhere inside. Carly looked up at Jack with huge, startled eyes.

"Do you have a cat?" he whispered.

She shook her head as she slowly rose to her feet.

"A dog?" he asked hopefully.

Licking her lips, she breathed, "Not even a hard-headed goldfish."

Jack noiselessly set his overnight bag and grocery sack onto the floor. "Don't move or make a sound," he commanded, pulling out his gun.

Carly emitted a choked exclamation of horror as she plastered herself against the wall. "Rule five," she gasped. "No guns!"

"Tell that to whoever is waiting inside." He curled his fingers around the doorknob and slowly began to turn it. At the sound of muffled footsteps from somewhere inside the apartment, every muscle in his body tensed for battle.

"Wait!" Carly gasped. She stepped toward him with a nervous glance at the closed door.

"Now what?" he hissed under his breath.

"I have to tell you a story."

It took Jack a moment to speak. "As fascinated as I am," he began, his voice tight and low, "by whatever significance your story has at this moment, it's going to have to wait. Now stand back."

"But this is important," she persisted. "When I was nine years old, I climbed this huge willow tree in our front yard. I almost made it to the very top.

When my three older brothers saw me, they panicked and started climbing up after me." She paused to take a breath. "I never asked to be rescued. But they insisted on coming after me anyway... *ordering* me to stay put. When my oldest brother fell off a branch and broke his ankle, the other two were too paranoid to move. I had to climb down and call the fire department."

"Is that it?" he asked tersely.

Carly looked up at him as if she had all the time in the world. "Do you know the moral of this story?"

"Your entire family is nuts?"

She rolled her eyes. "No. It means I'm not a helpless doll. Believe it or not, my brothers still haven't learned that lesson. They're always telling me what to do and how to do it. Treating me like some fragile piece of porcelain. I've actually had nightmares about being trapped in a china cabinet. That's why I moved all the way to Pine City. Three hundred miles just so I could run my own life."

Jack patiently waited for her mouth to stop moving. "Are you finished?" he asked.

"Yes."

"Good. Now stand back and be quiet."

She scowled at him. "There's no need to be rude." Heaving her purse over one shoulder, she took a deep breath and said, "I'm coming with you."

Jack ran his fingers frantically through his hair. "Are you out of your mind?"

She took another deep breath. "I'm not a patient person. I won't be able to stand waiting out here, not knowing what's happening. It's my apartment, after all. I have a right to be in on the bust. Maybe I can distract the intruder..."

Tempted as he was at this moment to send her in there *alone* to face the danger, Jack suppressed his rising exasperation and carefully replaced his gun in its holster. Then he grasped her by both shoulders and pushed her gently but firmly against the wall. Her long, silky curls brushed against the tops of his fingers. "Absolutely not," he growled. "You are to stay out here where it's safe. Remember rule number one?"

"No smoking of any kind," she quipped. "That includes guns. Would you rather just take a ride back down the elevator and call for backup?"

"Rule number one," he rasped, ignoring her suggestion, "is to do exactly as I tell you."

She blinked at him. "I never agreed to follow your rule."

Still pinning Carly to the wall, Jack groaned and dropped his head down in despair. He'd never survive the next four weeks with this woman. Even though her blue eyes reminded him of the summer sky and her lips looked dewy, moist, and delicious, she threatened his very sanity. And he'd known her less than an hour.

He decided to give it one more try. If he could just get into the apartment and apprehend the intruder, his problems might be over. If he caught the perpetrator of the anonymous note, maybe the district attorney would decide Carly didn't need protection anymore. At this precise moment, Jack preferred to take his chances with an armed suspect rather than the feisty woman in front of him.

"All I want to do is protect you," he stressed softly. "That's my job." He tightened his grasp on her shoulders when she opened her mouth to protest. "I admire your..." Jack searched for just the right word. *Stupidity* came to mind, but he doubted he'd win her over with that one. "...spirit, but I can't allow you to put yourself at risk. Now we can either both stand out here while your apartment is ransacked, or I can go in and check it out."

"Oh, all right," she grumbled. "I'll stay out here."

He breathed a sigh of relief. Finally. One more protest and he would have been provoked enough to take her into protective custody himself. They'd both be a lot safer if she spent the next four weeks in a secure location.

When this was all over, he intended to make it

clear to Trevor that he'd never sign up for a job with Cowboy Confidential again, unless it was an assignment to hunt down cattle rustlers or round up wild stallions. But first things first.

Jack reached once again for his gun just as the door to her apartment abruptly swung open.

2

"Don't shoot!" Carly's cry echoed down the hallway.

The woman standing in the doorway screamed and slammed the door in their faces. Carly barely got a glimpse of the green facial mask smeared over full cheeks and the pink electric rollers clipped in platinum hair.

She knew it. No deadly intruder awaited them. No psychotic assassin. Her heart still pounded in her chest and her knees felt weak and shaky. You witness one double murder and everybody around you starts overreacting. Like Jack Holden, barreling into her life, barking orders and waving his handgun around.

He might be drop-dead gorgeous, but she wanted to live a little while longer. At least long enough to find out why her childhood friend, Alma Jones, had shown up unexpectedly at her door. Or rather, on the other side of her door.

"Alma, open this door right now!" Carly shouted.

Jack lowered his gun. Then he looked over at Carly and scowled. "Friend of yours?"

With a curt nod she raised her hand and rapped her knuckles against the laminated veneer. "From North Bend, Texas. We grew up there together." She knocked again, harder this time, and yelled, "Alma, open up."

Without a word, Jack reached over and turned the key, which still protruded from the lock. When it clicked, he withdrew it and dropped it into his pocket. "After you," he said politely.

He was really beginning to annoy her.

Carly walked into the small living room to find Alma ripping the curlers out of her hair.

"Nice boyfriend you've got there, Carly," she cried. A blue-and-yellow-striped bathrobe covered most of her voluptuous form. Alma turned to Jack and opened her arms wide. "Why don't you just go ahead and shoot me? I'm unarmed. A helpless female. Do us both a favor."

She closed her eyes and threw her head back, the dried avocado mask cracking around her fleshy jawline. Alma's talent for drama had won her several awards and the role of Stella in North Bend High

School's rendition of *A Streetcar Named Desire.* At twenty-nine, she still loved playing to an audience.

Jack waved one hand in the air. "Howdy, I'm Jack. I just stopped by for a little visit with my favorite cousin." He draped his arm around Carly's shoulders. "Then it's on to Anchorage. You must be Alma."

Carly's skin tingled and her heart thumped against her chest as she stood in Jack's casual embrace. Turning her head away from him, she bristled at how snugly she fit beneath his arm.

Just like a stuffed doll.

Alma slowly lifted her head and opened eyes encircled by the avocado mask. The very picture of a nauseous raccoon. "That's a lie. I know all of her cousins." She folded her arms across her bathrobe and shook her head. "Men. This is so disgustingly typical." Her gaze moved to Carly. "What is he? Married?"

"I seriously doubt it," Carly replied, shrugging out from under Jack's arm and heading for the sofa. She needed to rally her frazzled nerves and figure out what to do with her very own gunslinger. He might be nice to look at, but his presentation needed a lot of work. The man could at least apologize for holding her friend at gunpoint.

But Jack didn't apologize. He cased her apartment with one long, assessing glance, then reached out to turn the lock on her door, the corners of his mouth curving in disapproval.

Alma grabbed her arm and pulled Carly down next to her on the sofa. "He makes me nervous," she whispered, nodding her head toward Jack.

"What are you doing here?" Carly asked. "What's going on?"

"You're asking *me* what's going on?" Alma gaped. "In case you didn't notice, Wyatt Earp here just pulled a gun on me. And he's probably married. Is this the kind of man you've been searching for? If I told your family..."

"We're not talking about me," Carly interrupted. "I want to know what you're doing in Pine City. You've never visited me here before. When you called me last week you didn't say a word about stopping by."

Alma shrugged her rounded shoulders. "I wanted to surprise you."

"It worked," Jack said, dropping into a thrift store armchair. Carly winced at the sound of his weight hitting the fragile wood.

"So how did you get into the apartment?" he asked briskly.

Alma stuck her chin out. "The super let me in after he rescued me from the elevator. I was stuck in that antiquated death trap for nearly twenty minutes!"

Jack's voice hardened. "He just *let* you into Carly's apartment?"

"Yeah," Alma retorted, "after I threatened to sue. Obviously, I don't look like the dangerous type." Her face crumpled, causing small clods of avocado to litter the floor and sofa. "He didn't even frisk me."

"Alma, what's wrong?" Carly asked, wondering what happened to her friend's lovely auburn locks and sweet nature. "I come home to find my best friend bitter and blond. What's the story, Alma? Come on, spill it."

"I already did," Alma confessed. "That orange stuff in your refrigerator is now in the wastebasket, along with the shattered remains of a pretty expensive-looking crystal serving dish." She winced, creating fissures along her cheeks and chin. "I'm really sorry."

"My pumpkin mousse," Carly groaned.

"If it's any consolation, it tasted absolutely delicious. Some of it fell into a bowl of spinach salad, so I got to sample it."

Carly groaned again. "So much for my good intentions. I wanted to convince my landlord to forgo, or at least postpone, this month's rent by serving him a little gourmet meal."

Alma reached over to pat her shoulder. "Don't worry. I scraped most of the mousse off the salad and then stirred it up really well, so the orange doesn't show. It looks as good as new."

"Did you touch her breasts?" Jack asked.

Alma stared at him in horror. "What are you, some kind of pervert?" She pulled the last roller from her head and tossed it onto the glass-topped coffee table. Her platinum curls protruded from her head like broken mattress springs.

"Who is this guy?" she whispered to Carly, tilting her head in Jack's direction. "I know he's handsome in a Neanderthal sort of way, but he's not your type at all."

"You don't understand..." Carly's gaze flickered to her new bodyguard. He didn't look happy. Too bad. She wasn't exactly overjoyed herself. Her feet throbbed in her high heels and the grimy film on her contact lenses was making her eyes itch and burn. She also had a sneaking suspicion that the avocado she'd saved to make guacamole was now nourishing Alma's facial pores.

"I don't *want* to understand," Alma countered. "I think you should dump him. Pronto. You deserve better than this."

Jack took off his cowboy hat and placed it on top of his overnight bag. Then he leaned his head back against the chair and closed his eyes. The metallic handle of his gun, strapped against his lean waist, gleamed in the sunlight.

"Believe me, I've thought about it," Carly replied under her breath.

"Carly, listen to me," Alma said earnestly. "I know you've been alone a long time, and some women might find a cowboy like him attractive. But take it from me, no man is worth it. Especially one with violent tendencies. I mean, he carries a gun." She rolled her eyes. "That's not one of *The Top Ten Traits of True Love.* Think about it. The guy actually *accused me* of touching your breasts. His insecurity must be phenomenal. Professor Frey always emphasizes the importance of..."

"Did you say Frey?" Jack interrupted, his gray eyes wide-open and as hard as flint. "As in Professor Chester Frey?"

Alma started, her hand fluttering to her throat. "Yes. That Professor Chester Frey. I know he's a homicidal maniac now, but he did write *The Top Ten Traits of True Love."* Her lower lip quivered. "I met my husband at one of his seminars." She buried her face in her hands and burst into tears. "It was love at first sight." Tiny rivulets of green saltwater ran through her fingers.

"Oh, Alma," Carly crooned, dabbing ineffectually

at the gooey green mess with a tissue. "Is this about Stanley? Are you two having problems?"

"Not anymore," Alma hiccupped between sobs. "I left him."

"When did all this happen?" Carly asked gently.

"Two days ago. I didn't know what to do or where to go. Your picture's been in the *North Bend Gazette* so much lately, what with the murder and all." She sniffed and took a deep breath. "They had a big article in there about it and all about your life in Pine City. How you run a successful catering business here and live life in the fast lane." Alma covered her face with a tissue. "While I've been stalled out in North Bend."

"Don't say that," Carly soothed, handing her the box of tissues and patting her lightly on the back. "You're just upset. You need time to sort out your feelings."

Alma swallowed her tears, then smiled wanly at Carly. "Do you mind if I stay here with you? Just for a little while?"

"Of course not," Carly told her. "You're welcome to stay as long as you like."

Alma sniffed as she looked around the apartment. "It's not exactly like your mother described it. I thought you lived in a fancy penthouse."

Carly cleared her throat. "I might have exaggerated a little in my emails to her. You know how she worries." She looked over at Jack, frowning when she saw his eyes narrow with suspicion as he stared at Alma.

"You never said exactly why you left your husband," he prodded.

Alma sighed. "After what happened with Professor Frey, I... just felt like our whole marriage was based on a lie."

Jack nodded thoughtfully. "So Professor Frey brought you to Pine City?"

"I didn't say that," Alma said defensively.

"Obviously Professor Frey's crime affected you quite a bit," he said, his gaze intense on her green face.

Carly grimaced. A paranoid bodyguard and amateur psychoanalyst all rolled up into one.

Alma sniffed. "I think it was finding Stanley having cybersex that really did it. I suppose I should have seen it coming. He told me the Hotcakes website he kept visiting was for a pancake house franchise he was interested in." She looked forlornly at Carly. "Don't you think North Bend could use a pancake house?"

"It could use a lot of things," Carly replied, certain her sleepy hometown was buzzing about this

Hotcakes website scandal. No wonder Alma wanted to escape.

"Anyway, I believed him. I thought owning a business might put some sizzle into our marriage. Into our lives." She tore another tissue from the box. "I told him we could be just like Carly. Be our own boss. Lead an exciting life, even if we still lived in North Bend." She twisted the tissue between her fingers. "I was so excited I went to the website one day myself, you know, just to find out some more information..."

Carly closed her eyes, just imagining what her friend learned.

"No pancake house?" Jack asked.

"No pancake house," Alma repeated dully. "So that's it. I'm through with Stanley and I'm through with North Bend."

"All this time I thought you were so happy," Carly said.

Alma sniffed again. "I thought Stanley could make me happy. He's so handsome and charming. According to Professor Frey's love chart, we're a perfect match."

Jack leaned forward in his chair, his elbows resting on his knees. "Sounds like you're a big fan of the professor's."

Alma's mouth tightened. "I don't want to talk about it anymore."

"Why?" Jack hammered. "Do you have something to hide?"

"Jack," Carly broke in sharply, "that's enough." She glared at him, then nodded toward Alma, who was once again weeping into her tissue.

Alma took a couple of deep, broken breaths and wiped her face, streaking avocado into her freshly washed hair. "No, it's all right. I don't have anything to hide."

"You've answered enough of his questions," Carly told her. Seeing Jack scowl with annoyance suddenly made her feel much better. "Now answer one of mine."

"My hair?" Alma guessed.

Carly tried to be tactful. "What in the world happened to it?"

"I dyed it because I want a fresh start. I'm going to lose a few pounds and find a great job..."

"Become a new person?" Jack suggested. "Do you sometimes feel like you're two different people? Do you ever hear voices?"

Alma narrowed her eyes. "Only the one telling me that all men are jerks. That's loud and clear."

"Jack isn't a jerk on purpose," Carly said, hoping it was true. "He's just doing his job."

"What is that exactly?" Alma asked. "Guard dog?"

"Close," Carly said. "He's my new bodyguard."

Alma gaped as she looked from Carly to Jack and back again. "Why on earth do you need a cowboy bodyguard?"

"It's just until the trial," Carly said. "The district attorney called it a necessary precaution."

"So does that mean he'll be staying here?" Alma asked. "With us?"

"With Carly," Jack amended. "I'm here to protect her from harm."

Alma looked him up and down. "So who's going to protect her from you?"

Carly stood up, wincing as her shoes pinched her toes. "He'll only be here four weeks."

"Unless Frey gets another postponement," Jack said. His piercing gray eyes met Carly's. Swallowing hard, she sat back down on the sofa.

"You two are spending day and night together for four weeks?" Alma looked between the two of them. "Are you sure this is strictly business?"

"Of course," Carly replied, with much more bravado than she felt. "Jack is simply protecting my body, not taking possession of it." She licked her dry lips. "He's a professional. Simply here to do his job. Right?"

"Right," he affirmed. "I'd never compromise Carly's safety, or my career, by crossing that boundary.

As long as she obeys my rules, the next few weeks should proceed smoothly."

At the word *obey,* Carly's stomach tightened. *Fat chance.* Despite Jack's rather arrogant and commanding tone, she refused to become a prisoner in her own home. Maybe if he shaved, and got rid of his gun, and lost that lean, hungry look in his molten gray eyes she'd let him stay. But she'd never let him rule over her.

Alma emitted a snort of laughter. "Smoothly? I'll believe *that* when I see it."

"You're nuts," Carly snapped. "It isn't Alma."

Jack glanced over at the closed bathroom door where he heard Alma singing off-key in the shower. "How can you be so sure?"

Gathering up the wadded tissues scattered across the sofa and floor, she replied, "Because I've known her forever and she isn't the poison pen type. Or should I say, poison crayon."

"All right. I won't argue with you." He moved a step closer to her and lowered his voice. "But you can't let her stay here."

Carly brushed her hair off her face. "Why not?"

"Well, in the first place, I'm not certain she's stable," he said carefully.

"That's ridiculous," she scoffed. "Alma's as sane as I am."

Jack let that one go by. "In the second place, I need to maintain security around here. Your life may be in danger." He went on, despite the skeptical expression on her face. "The super's letting people into your apartment without your permission. That lock on your door is about as reliable as a dime-store toy. And I doubt those guys hanging around on the street corner belong to the Neighborhood Watch Association. Keeping you safe will be hard enough without your friend Alma living here with us."

"But you heard what she's going through. Her marriage might be over. How can I abandon her at a time like this?"

Jack shrugged, feeling as alien and helpless as ever when it came to affairs of the heart. "You don't have to just dump her. Find her a support group. Call a shrink. Anything. It's not as if splitting up is so unusual. At least it's better than clinging to a relationship that might turn abusive or violent."

"Sophie Odell split up with Professor Frey and look what happened." Her blue eyes darkened with sadness. "I call filling your lover with lead both abusive and violent."

"Love can be... dangerous," he said. "My brother Nick is a cop and sees the results of it every day in domestic dispute calls, stalkings..."

His mind suddenly flashed back to twenty-four years ago, when his grandparents broke the awful news to Jack and his brothers that their parents had been killed in a car accident. He'd never seen Grandpa Henry cry before that moment and the memory was as clear and crisp as if it just happened yesterday. So was the pain.

Jack blinked back the memory. "In my opinion," he said roughly, "love isn't worth the risk. The more people you love, the more you have to lose."

Carly stared thoughtfully at him for a moment and then shrugged. "Maybe you're right. I know too many couples who aren't living happily ever after."

Surprised at the unexpected agreement, Jack watched in silence as she picked up the small bits of avocado dotting the sofa. She moved with an unconscious grace. As she bent forward, her hair fell softly against the creamy smoothness of her cheeks. Keeping an eye on her for the next four weeks would be no problem. Taking his eyes off her would be the challenge. He tested himself, forcing his gaze to wander around the rest of the room.

It was spotless. He marveled again at the difference between it and the rest of the dilapidated building.

Her floors were bare of carpet, the natural hardwood flooring swept clean and polished to a rich, golden brown. A wide variety of lush green houseplants filled the room, thriving on the windowsills and in every nook and cranny. Golden sunlight streamed through the gauzy ivory drapes adorning the windows. The sofa and armchair were worn but upholstered in the same sky-blue damask and made cozy by an assortment of gingham throw pillows. Nothing looked new or expensive. Just very tasteful and very clean.

He liked her sense of style. Soon, he'd have his own home to decorate, since he'd recently purchased a nice piece of land that already had a barn and two-story house on it. He even had a small herd of cattle grazing there. His dream was to build and maintain his own cattle ranch someday, just like Grandpa Henry had done.

There was something about this apartment that reminded him of the family home on Elk Creek Ranch—a warmth and a coziness that you couldn't buy in any store. Grandma Hattie put her whole heart into that home and her grandsons. Carly had done the same with her place, using a special touch to make it airy and bright and optimistic about the future.

His gaze fell back on Carly. Something inside of him recoiled at the notion that she might not have a future. Jack steeled himself against that possibility. He'd see to it that she survived this ordeal and lived on to drive some other man crazy.

Carly straightened up and squared her shoulders. "I'm not asking Alma to leave. She's my friend and she needs me." Tossing the avocado crumbs into a wastebasket, she marched toward the kitchen.

He followed her, grabbing his sack of groceries on the way. His stomach had been growling ever since he heard about the untimely demise of the pumpkin mousse. He couldn't fight crime or Carly on an empty stomach.

"The way I see it," he said, unloading his groceries onto the counter, "Alma needs protection almost as much as you do. I assume the only reason you two survived this long is because your hometown of North Bend is crime-free."

He looked up to see Carly staring at him. "What's wrong?"

"I don't need protection. I'm perfectly capable of taking care of myself."

Jack laughed. "Carly, you're a dreamer. This place

is a thief's paradise. No dead bolt, no security alarm, not even a ferocious lap dog."

"I've got you now."

He studied her for a moment, trying to decide if he'd just been insulted. She looked up at him with her big, blue eyes full of innocence.

"Right," he said warily. "You've got me now. But I won't be here forever."

"Promise?"

Jack wadded up the paper sack. So she didn't want him. Fine. He was only here to keep her safe, not win a popularity contest. He still had four weeks to verse her in the fine art of self-defense. In the meantime, he needed to gain her trust.

"Nice kitchen," he observed. "Where's your stove?"

"You're standing next to it."

Jack looked down at the gleaming steel contraption on his right. "This thing?"

She walked over and slid her hand across its shiny surface, like a model demonstrating a product on a game show. "Isn't it beautiful? This range is the top of the line. Did you notice the cast iron grates and the sealed burners? It even has a built-in spice rack."

"It's gorgeous," he quipped. "But I'll take curtain number three."

"You just don't know state-of-the-art equipment when you see it," she replied. Then she proceeded to show off her heavy-duty food processor, complete with a blender attachment and dough hooks... the triple stainless-steel sink she installed herself... and enough shiny copper pans hanging from a rack to cook up plenty of grub for every cowboy on a cattle drive.

"I'd love a walk-in refrigerator," she told him, an enthusiastic sparkle in her blue eyes, "but that will have to wait until I'm in a place of my own." She sighed. "All this stuff wasn't cheap. For now, I just need to concentrate on building up my business clientele."

Then she moved on to the utensil drawer.

"This is all very interesting," Jack lied, after he learned how to work the garlic press. "But I'm starving. How about supper? To celebrate our first night together." He could have kicked himself as soon as the words left his mouth. *Their first night together.* That sounded intimate. Provocative. Dangerous. Maybe he needed a bodyguard, too.

"Can you cook?" she asked.

"Of course." He waved to the food lined up on the counter. His staples. Twenty boxes of macaroni and cheese. A case of instant soup. Ten packages of hot dogs.

Carly backed up against the refrigerator. "That is atrocious."

"No," he countered cheerfully, reaching for a box of macaroni, "it's delicious. I've learned how to survive with only one essential culinary skill."

"Boiling water?" she guessed.

"I'm quite good at it, too," Jack said as he reached overhead and grabbed a small copper pan off the rack.

"That's a flan pan," Carly said, taking it out of his hands and replacing it on a hook.

Jack reached for another pan just as her cell phone rang on the counter. He glanced over at the screen, but instead of seeing a name or phone number, the word "Unknown" appeared.

"Don't answer it," he ordered as she moved toward it. "Let it go to voicemail."

Carly momentarily froze, her mouth turned down at the corners as another shrill ring rent the air.

"This is silly," she snapped, reaching for her cell phone.

"Wait!" Alma cried, running into the kitchen with a fuzzy pink towel wrapped around her head. "Don't answer it." Her hand fluttered to her throat. "It might be Stanley."

"He knows you're here with Carly?" Jack asked.

Alma shrugged. "Well, yeah, sort of. I left him a

note. You don't know Stanley. He'd be worried sick if I just disappeared. He's always warning me about all the perverts in the world. If I didn't tell him I went to Carly's, he'd probably call the state patrol."

"No wonder you left him," Carly mused.

"Once I was late coming home from the mall and a cop pulled me over," Alma recalled. "Stanley had reported me as a missing person."

Jack saw Carly shudder.

"He always made me feel so loved," Alma said with a sigh. The phone rang again. "But I don't want to talk to him. I'm not ready."

"Nobody answers Carly's cell phone unless she recognizes the name or number on the screen," Jack commanded. "Otherwise, just let calls go to voicemail."

"But it might be a customer," Carly argued. "This is my phone. My apartment. I do have a business to run..." Her voice trailed off as the cell phone went silent. A few moments later, she picked it up and played the voicemail on speaker.

"Hey, Carly," crooned a tenor voice across the telephone line. "This is Big Bob from station KUTY. We got those customers you've been craving." He chuckled. "Our top three finalists in the Dial-a-Dinner contest. We got a great response and all the winners agreed to your stipulations."

"Listen, babe," he said, his disc jockey voice dropping to a seductive growl, "if you want to experiment on a willing victim, just give me a call. I think we could cook up a hot night together."

"Yuck," Alma said, after the voicemail ended. Then she padded back to the bathroom.

Jack counted silently to ten. Then he counted again. "So, *babe*," he began, still straining to control his temper, "what, exactly, is the Dial-a-Dinner contest?"

Carly cleared her throat. "It's a new marketing strategy for Carly's Creations. I told you I need to build up my clientele."

"Free catering?"

She nodded. "For three lucky winners. Of course, I had to set a limit on the value. I can't afford to pay for a banquet. Just small, simple affairs."

"You're not serious?"

"Totally. Oh, and I think you should know there's a time limit, too. The offer expires in one month."

Jack unclenched his jaw. "You told the district attorney you didn't have any catering jobs."

Carly opened a drawer and pulled out a crisply folded apron. "I never actually said that."

"You implied it."

She shook out the apron and tied it around her

waist. "All that doesn't matter now anyway. I think we need to talk."

Jack set down the box of macaroni. "I agree." It was time Carly Weiss took him seriously. "Do you have a dictionary?"

She looked up at him in confusion. "A dictionary?"

"I want you to look up the word *dangerous*," he told her, folding his arms across his chest. "Because you obviously do not know the meaning of the word. Then I want you to call up your favorite disc jockey, Big Bob, and tell him the Dial-a-Dinner deal is off."

"I can't do that."

"All right," Jack conceded, struggling to keep his composure. "Then postpone it. Until after the trial."

"No way." She reached into the refrigerator, pulling out a carton of eggs and a bag of plums. "I've got a reputation to think about. A business like mine thrives or dies on referrals. I can't just cancel without a good reason."

He didn't know whether to laugh or grab her by the shoulders and give her a good shake. So, he just stood there calmly and said, "I can think of several good reasons. Some lunatic out there wants you dead, for one."

Carly blinked at him. "We don't know that for sure." He threw his hands up in the air. "We might not know it *for sure* until you're lying on a coroner's table. Can you afford to take that chance?"

Sparks fired in her indigo eyes. "What I can't afford is sitting idly by while my business goes under. Do you want to drive me to bankruptcy? I'm already teetering on the brink."

The heated flush in her cheeks made her even more lovely to look at. Jack wrenched his gaze away and stared hard at the toaster.

"The odds that one of the winners of the Dial-a-Dinner contest is the person you're looking for are... astronomical," she continued. "Maybe you better just stay home with Alma while I'm working. You're much too paranoid. I can't have you fingerprinting my clients during the first course."

Stay home with Alma? Even more amazing was the fact that she looked completely serious. Jack drew a deep breath and spoke very slowly. "As long as we don't know who we're looking for, everybody is a suspect. I intend to be your shadow for the next four weeks. You won't make a move without me."

Carly shook her head, her jaw set at a stubborn angle. "I can't allow it."

Drawing himself up to his full six foot three inches, he squared his shoulders and said, "Just try and stop me." He'd never actually challenged a woman with his physical presence before, but he didn't know what else to do. Especially when Carly refused to listen to reason.

She looked up at him, blinked three times, and then whirled around to face the counter. "Ahhh," she moaned.

Her cry ripped through him like a knife. He wanted to scare her into submission, not sobs. He watched helplessly as she hunched over the counter, her head down, her shoulders stiff.

A woman's tears always made him uncomfortable. But Carly's rendered him speechless. She was so full of sass and spunk; she was the last woman on earth he expected to succumb to weeping when she didn't get her way. He reached out a tentative hand to console her, gently caressing her soft, silky hair.

"Don't... touch me," she murmured, her back still to him.

Guilt tore at him as he drew his hand away from her. "All right," he grumbled, ready to give in, ready to do almost anything to stop this quiet torture. Telling himself that protecting her was really all that mattered. "You can cater the Dial-a-Dinner winners without any interference from me." He ran his fingers through his hair, wishing she'd turn around and yell at him... kick him... anything but assault him with this weapon he feared most. "Your safety is still my main concern," he said, "but I'll try to stay out of your way as much as possible."

He watched her take a deep breath and with one finger, carefully wipe the moisture from underneath her right eye.

"Will you work as my assistant so nobody guesses the real reason you're hanging around me?" she asked, her voice tight and low.

"Fine," he agreed desperately. "I'll do whatever you want." He heard her delicate sniff. "Do you feel better now?"

She carefully touched two fingers to her right eye and pulled out a wafer-thin contact lens. A soft sigh of relief passed her lips.

"Contact attack," she said, setting the removed lens in a clean ceramic spoon rest. Then she turned to face him, her eyes clear and shining with triumph. "I do feel much better now."

Reaching into a drawer, she pulled out another apron and handed it to Jack.

He took it and held it at arm's length.

"It's not radioactive," she said with an amused smile.

"What am I supposed to do with it?"

"Put it on." Carly flipped open her bulky recipe file. "If you're going to act as my assistant, we have to make it believable."

“I never...” he began, fingering delicate white lace. Then he realized what he’d agreed to while Carly was in the midst of her painful, eye-watering, coercive contact attack.

He stared in horror at the very white, very feminine apron. Surely this went above and beyond the call of duty.

Carly smiled brightly up at him. “Now about your gun...”

3

He looked good enough to eat.

Dressed in black slacks and a crisply pressed white dress shirt, Jack emanated the simple but elegant style she'd always dreamed of for Carly's Creations. After six relentless days of haggling over that apron and an offer to pay the expenses, he finally convinced her to try a new look. The black bow tie definitely added a touch of class. Her own uniform matched his, except for the delicate crocheted lace trimming her collar and cuffs.

Carly wiped her damp palms nervously against her sheer black apron as she watched Jack pick up the round serving tray and once again attempt to balance it in the air above his head. The heat from the oven in the clubhouse kitchen warmed the room to an almost unbearable temperature. The dance music was so loud it was vibrating the platters of hors d'oeuvres lined up on the counter.

"Just relax," she said as the tray wobbled on the palm of his hand. One stuffed mushroom rolled off the top, bouncing against his shoulder before falling to the linoleum floor.

"Another kamikaze mushroom dies for fungi everywhere," he quipped.

Carly grabbed a damp dishcloth and dabbed out the spot of red sauce on his broad shoulder. This cowboy might be a disaster as a waiter, but it only made matters worse when he didn't take the job seriously. "Let's try it again," she said, her patience wearing thin.

"Can't we just set the trays on the buffet table and be done with it?" he grumbled as another mushroom hit the top of his head and skimmed off his nose. "We've killed half a dozen mushrooms already."

"You've killed them. I've just presided over their burial down the garbage disposal. And in answer to your question, absolutely not." Carly stood on her tiptoes to pick a piece of onion out of his hair. "And no buffet table, the client wants silver platter service."

Jack lowered the tray to the kitchen counter just as another mushroom took a dive. He caught it deftly in a lean hand and then popped it into his mouth.

"Too much cayenne pepper," he said, chewing thoughtfully.

Carly blew a lock of hair off her face. "As if I'd take the advice of a man who considers fried pork rinds a delicacy."

"This from a woman who has never even tasted one. Where is your adventurous spirit?"

She shuddered. "Please. I suffer enough watching you eat those things."

"That, I believe." A slow grin stretched one corner of his mouth. "You couldn't take your eyes off me and my bag of pork rinds yesterday afternoon. You wanted one. Admit it."

"Never." Carly rinsed the dishcloth under the tap. "I just wanted to be ready in case you dropped dead of a heart attack. I could actually hear your arteries clogging. Cholesterol kills, you know."

"So do deranged fans who make creepy threats. But I don't see that stopping you. In case you haven't noticed, you've got bigger worries than a bag of pork rinds."

Glancing at the slim gold watch on her wrist, she nodded. "You're right. It's time to start serving." She ignored the shadow of annoyance that crossed his face. "Now, do you remember everything I told you?"

"No, my mind went blank as soon as you made me

put on this bow tie. I think it's cutting off all the blood to my head."

"Stop complaining." Picking up the tray of appetizers, she shoved it into his hands, safely at waist level. "Waiting tables isn't rocket science. Just remember to always use the tongs whenever you handle the hors d'oeuvres, to speak politely, and that the customer is always right."

"Even if that customer wants to kill the caterer?" Jack asked dryly.

"We've been over this," Carly said, wiping her hands on a dish towel. "This is a roomful of sorority sisters. I'm in no danger."

"If I had a dime for every time I've heard you say that in the last week, I could buy my horse ranch." He frowned down at the row of colorful trays on the counter. "Maybe even quit moonlighting as a waiter."

"I just wish you'd start believing it."

"It doesn't matter if I believe it. I've been hired to protect you until the trial, and I intend to do just that."

"Which explains the security check when we first arrived?"

"Get used to it," he admonished her.

"Did you find any maniacs hiding under the table? Or assassins lurking in the toilet stalls? Assault weapons planted in the potted palms?" Carly tried not to laugh at the disgruntled expression on his handsome face. "Maybe one of the sorority sisters in there is really Professor Frey in disguise. Did you check for whiskers?"

Jack's only reply was a disgusted grunt of exasperation as he steadied the tray in his hands and then pushed his way through the swinging door. Raucous feminine laughter rose and then fell as the door swung shut behind him.

The buzzing of the oven timer turned Carly's attention to her cheese puffs. Crisp and golden, she pulled them from the oven, their delicate, tangy aroma filling the air. Her eyes watered from the heat and the beauty of her creation. Perfect. Tonight, she'd settle for nothing less. Her first Dial-a-Dinner contest winner was none other than Sidra Collins, daughter of one of Pine City's most successful entrepreneurs.

Sidra was in charge of the bachelorette party for one of her Alpha Chi sisters. Finicky down to the last fettucine, the woman spent days scrutinizing Carly's diverse menu lists. After changing her mind at least five times, she finally selected a menu of assorted gourmet hors d'oeuvres. Still not completely satisfied, Sidra insisted that goat cheese be substituted for Brie and that the shrimp marinate in an expensive French

Chablis instead of a California domestic for the seafood kabobs.

Carly carefully lifted each cheese puff off the baking sheet and set them on the warming tray. Then she picked up the decorator's tube and piped caviar into hollowed pea pods, artfully arranging the finished product on a serving platter. By the time she'd received Sidra's list, she'd barely had time to prepare the food. Surprisingly, Jack's help proved invaluable. When he put his gun away, the man was almost friendly. Except for those annoying rules of his.

At least he didn't make a bad roommate. She found she even liked the masculine touch he brought to her home. A lost television remote control, wet towels in the laundry hamper, dark whiskers in her sink. Even the incessant drone of televised baseball on Sunday afternoon.

To her surprise and relief, she sensed Jack relaxing a little more as each day passed without additional threats or imminent signs of danger. A faint blush warmed her cheeks as she thought of the anonymous letter she'd received in today's mail. The letter she hid under her mattress.

The few lines of verse were as innocuous and uninformative as the poem she'd read in the district attorney's office. The paper was the same lavender, unlined stationery. But instead of a crayon sketch, the only picture was of grisly skull and crossbones, rubber-stamped with black ink in one corner.

Rushing to prepare for the party, she'd had neither the time nor the inclination to show it to Jack. He still didn't realize the importance of impressing such potential future customers as Sidra Collins and her high-society crowd. He might even add another rule to his collection—forbidding her to cater. So she'd decided what Jack didn't know wouldn't hurt him. Or Carly's Creations.

Her cowboy bodyguard breezed back through the kitchen door, accompanied by a cacophony of shrill whistles and slurred propositions. If she looked past his smothering protectiveness and by-the-book mentality, Carly had to admit that Jack gave an unexpected boost to her business. His good looks and tall, brawny frame definitely pleased the guests of this evening's affair.

"They want another pitcher of margaritas," he said, setting an empty pitcher into the sink. "They don't need it, but..."

"But we aim to please," Carly concluded, handing him a full, frosted pitcher with strawberries floating on the top.

"You go out there this time," he said, setting the

pitcher on the counter. "I'll stay in the kitchen where it's safe."

Carly laughed, her hands on her hips. "This is a switch. I thought you were here to protect me."

"That's before I went out there alone. You're lucky I'm still in one piece. Those women are hungry for more than gourmet food." His smile faded. "Besides, Princess Sidra requests an audience with you. Immediately."

"Why? Did something happen?" Small talons of dread gripped her as Jack heaved a troubled sigh.

"There was an... incident."

"Oh, no! Jack, what happened? What did you do?"

A muscle twitched in his square jaw. "Just what you asked. I served the stuffed mushrooms, dropping three on the carpet, two on the tablecloth, and one into the wineglass of the hostess." He held up the silver serving tongs, clicking the tapered ends together. "That's when these came in quite handy."

Carly closed her eyes in mortification. "Please tell me you're joking."

"Everyone at the table found it amusing."

"Except Sidra, I'm sure. Jack, how could you do this to me?"

"All I did was follow your orders. That concept may seem foreign to you, but most of the time it works quite well." He cleared his throat as he set the tongs on the counter. "This just didn't happen to be one of those times."

"My orders?" she echoed, flabbergasted. "I don't recall asking you to improvise with the tongs."

"No, but you did say to use them whenever I handled the hors d'oeuvres."

Carly gritted her teeth. "All right. New orders. Use the tongs to only handle the hors d'oeuvres. Not to dip them into the customer's wineglass—or anywhere else. Is that clear?"

"Perfectly."

Brushing a few lone breadcrumbs off her black slacks, Carly mentally prepared herself for an unhappy client. "Time for some damage control. Just cross your fingers that Sidra doesn't fire us on the spot. This isn't exactly the kind of publicity I want to generate for my business." Jack held both hands in the air, his fingers spread wide apart. "Is that another order?"

She looked straight into his steely-gray eyes. "Remember when the D.A. promised me you'd inconvenience my life as little as possible?" She didn't wait for his reply. "Well, I'm finding you not only inconvenient, but irritating as well. Like this morning when you woke me up at seven a.m. to do a bed check."

"For your information, I exercised great restraint by not barging in on you half an hour earlier, when I first heard those suspicious noises coming from your room. It sounded like a herd of wild horses stampeding through your apartment."

Carly grimaced. "Alma is taking her calisthenics routine very seriously. She paid for it, though."

"I know." Jack shook his head. "I heard her scream when she turned on the shower. Remind me to thank Mrs. Kolinski in the downstairs apartment."

"Forget about Mrs. Kolinski. I'm worried about Sidra. Was she upset about your tongs in her wine?"

He pursed his lips. "Hard to tell. She's always got that look on her face."

"What look?"

"Like she just stepped in a cow pie with her designer shoes."

Carly squared her shoulders. "Well, let's at least be optimistic. Go ahead and warm up the pesto while I see to Sidra." Her gaze rested thoughtfully on his face. "And please try to stay out of trouble."

Jack picked up a wooden spoon and moved to the stove top. "Your wish is my command."

Carly smiled grimly as she moved toward the door. "Keep that in mind. I might make a wish sooner than you think."

Jack spotted trouble as soon as Carly breezed back through the kitchen door of the clubhouse. She smiled so disingenuously at him that the hairs prickled on the back of his neck. He'd seen that look on her face before.

"I took care of everything," she exclaimed. "The good news is that Sidra wasn't all that upset about the stuffed mushroom incident."

"And the bad news?" Jack inquired, more than a little suspicious of that conniving gleam in her blue eyes.

"The party's not going as well as she planned."

"Does that mean we're through here?" he asked hopefully. "Shall I start packing up?"

Carly moved a step closer to him. "Actually, they want more."

"More what?" He reached for a platter full of appetizers with a resigned sigh. After the incident with the tongs, he didn't relish going out there for another opportunity to screw up. "Dim sum? Cheese puffs? Pistachio tarts?"

Carly took a deep breath. "More you."

The tray tilted, causing half of the cheese puffs to roll onto the floor. She reached over and gently took the tray out of his hands. "The stripper canceled and the bride-to-be thinks you're awfully cute..."

"Wait just a minute," Jack said, backing up with

both hands stretched out before him to ward off her pursuit. "I've chopped onions for you. Diced ham. Shelled and ground nuts by hand." His retreat was halted by the refrigerator. "Even let you experiment on me with that vinegar sauce you created. Don't I deserve a little respect?"

"I do respect you," she said, reaching up to loosen his bow tie.

Jack grasped her hands and held them tightly in his own. "This isn't part of my assignment."

"I never wanted a bodyguard in the first place, so the least you could do is cooperate. Or shall I call D.A. Boyle and tell her you're not performing to my satisfaction?"

"Performing what?" he scoffed. "A striptease? Suppose our situations were reversed? You can't tell me you'd go out there into a roomful of ogling men and..." His gaze fell to the row of pearl buttons on her blouse and he lost his train of thought. "Forget it."

"But aren't you already working undercover as a waiter?"

"Yes," he replied tightly. "But the word is *under-cover,* not *without cover.* I might even consider it if the occasion demanded it. But the only one demanding it now is you." He set his jaw at a stubborn angle. "I'm sorry, but I'm declining your crazy offer. My job doesn't include stripping for a roomful of salivating women."

Carly nibbled her lower lip. "What if you don't actually have to strip?"

His gut tightened at the note of negotiation in her voice. "I don't actually *have* to do anything," he returned, "except keep you from harm until the trial."

"What if," she continued, slowly tugging at one end of his bow tie, "we compromise?"

Jack didn't know how to make his position any clearer. Didn't this woman realize how much he'd already compromised just to keep her happy? Waiting tables... putting up with Alma... wearing this stupid bow tie. And the things he *hadn't* done just to accommodate her. Like enforcing a curfew or insisting that Alma leave. Enough was enough. He was determined to stick to his guns on this issue. As if he'd ever consider agreeing to her outlandish proposal.

Then he made a strategic mistake. He looked down into the deep pools of her soft-indigo eyes. Their swirling depths caught and held him. He felt his resolve slipping like a life preserver out of his hands.

"A compromise?" he breathed, his senses whirling. She moved so close to him that he could see the tiny flutter at the base of her throat. He stood there mesmerized by the sight, and by the subtle scents of vanilla and cinnamon that lingered in her hair. A hunger stirred in him that no food could satisfy. His nostrils flared as her slender fingers brushed against his neck, then rested lightly on the collar of his shirt.

Deftly slipping one button out of its buttonhole, she murmured, "Let's just give Sidra and her sorority sisters a glimpse of your fabulous physique." Her fingers fell to the second button.

Jack's breath caught in his throat at her delicate touch. "My fabulous physique?" he echoed softly.

A smile played about her pink lips. "Sidra is wild about tall, dark, and dangerous." Carly slid her hands down to the third button of his shirt. Her soft, warm breath caressed his bare chest.

"And what's your opinion?"

Carly's gaze fell to the fourth button of his shirt as she teased it from the buttonhole. A rosy blush bloomed on her cheeks. "You know I believe the customer is always right," she said huskily. "But the Cottonwood Cooking Academy taught us to always leave them wanting a little more. So instead of a stripper, what if we give them a topless waiter?"

Jack surrendered without another word. He couldn't stop Carly if he wanted to, which he didn't. He closed his eyes as she gently tugged his shirt out from under his waistband. He stifled a groan as she pushed the shirt off his shoulders, her fingernails raking gently over his back.

"I'm sorry," she whispered, "did I hurt you?"

"No," he breathed. The sensation of Carly touching him surpassed any fantasy he'd ever imagined. Her fingers moved like quicksilver over hot iron.

He opened his eyes to see her neatly folding his shirt.

"Take out the pitcher of margaritas first," she said briskly. "Then we'll serve the cheese puffs while they're still warm."

Jack took a deep breath as the cold blast from the open refrigerator hit his overheated skin. "I can't believe I'm doing this."

"I know," she replied, beaming up at him. "Isn't catering fun?"

"You can't get rid of me," Jack said, sitting down at the breakfast table the next morning. He reached for the cereal box and filled his bowl to the brim.

"And you can't tell me what to do." Carly sat across from him, her hands wrapped around her steaming teacup. Her chestnut hair hung in damp tendrils around her freshly washed face. She tried to focus on her justified indignation and not on the play of muscles underneath his black T-shirt. The sight of shirtless Jack Holden last evening had outdone her vivid imagination. And she'd only seen half of him. *Just enough to leave her wanting more.*

"Obviously." He poured chocolate milk into his cereal bowl and then picked up his spoon. "You certainly didn't listen to me last night when I told you not to call the fire department." Jack crunched noisily on his mouthful of cereal and then swallowed. "The fire extinguisher put out that little blaze in no time. I told you there was no reason to panic."

"Right. So instead of apologizing, you had to say I told you so."

"Apologize?" He looked up at her, genuinely puzzled. "For what?"

Her eyes widened. "Where should I begin?" She ticked off each offense with a flick of her fingers. "Insulting Sidra Collins, which ruined any chance for future business with her or her wealthy friends. Dropping that bowl of salsa on the clubhouse carpet, which guaranteed I won't get one dime of my deposit returned. Torching the clubhouse kitchen... Need I go on?"

"You talk as if I burned down the place. The smoke got a little thick, but..."

"I know what happened," she interrupted. "I was

there. The smoke alarms wailed for an hour. The indoor sprinkler system activated and drenched everything and everybody. Including all the leftovers that I planned to live on for the next week!"

"If that's what you're upset about, stop worrying." Jack popped open the tab on his grape soda. "I told you I don't mind sharing my food with you if money's a little tight right now."

"Please," she groaned, shielding her eyes with one hand. "I can barely stand watching *you* eat it."

He shrugged, scooping up another spoonful of cereal. "It's your loss."

"Exactly," she retorted, wrapping the collar of her pink silk bathrobe more snugly around her shoulders. "My loss. My business. After that stunt you pulled last night, I'll be lucky if Sidra Collins doesn't sue Carly's Creations for damages."

Jack reached for the cereal box and refilled his bowl. "What more do you want from me? I served the appetizers. I poured margaritas. I even waited tables topless."

A deep sigh of exasperation escaped her lips. "I'm talking about the margaritas you poured for Sidra. A whole pitcher full, right over the top of her head!"

"She deserved it."

"I disagree. Besides, I thought you lived by rules.

What about the most important one in catering? The customer is always right."

Jack set down his spoon. "She grabbed my butt and then attempted to strip off my pants. For your information, I don't take kindly to anyone grabbing me without permission."

Carly tossed her paper napkin onto the table. "Thanks for the warning."

The subtle scent of her floral shampoo lingered in the air between them. Jack's gaze swept over her dark, curling hair to the soft roses in her cheeks as he wondered if there might not be an exception to that particular rule. What would he do if Carly walked over and grabbed him right now? Douse her with his grape soda? He forced his gaze back to the cereal crackling in his bowl. *Only if he knew what was good for him.*

"Then when I finally got Sidra all dried off and calmed down," she continued, "you had to make matters worse by setting the kitchen on fire." Her tone erased any apprehension on his part that she might attempt to grab him.

"Look," he said gruffly, growing irritated by her persistence as well as his increasing attraction to her, "I was simply following orders. You told me to turn up the burner under the crepes."

"Yes," Carly admitted, sparks flying in her eyes. "But I didn't tell you to add the cognac."

"They looked dry."

"They looked perfect until you flambéed them to the point of incineration."

"That fire could have been contained," Jack argued, forgetting his promise to himself not to blame Carly for the incident, "if you wouldn't have rushed into the kitchen and tried to smother the flames with your dish towel. The same one you used to dry off Sidra. The one soaked with *inflammable alcohol* from the margaritas."

Carly lifted her chin. "Which only proves my point. If you wouldn't have overreacted by dumping that pitcher on Sidra in the first place, none of this would have happened."

The chilly impasse between them was broken only by the chime of the doorbell.

"Expecting anyone?" Jack asked coolly.

"No," Carly replied, rising from her chair and moving toward the door. "Unless you called the fire marshal and reported me as an arsonist."

"Don't tempt me," Jack said, following her into the living room. "Putting you behind bars would certainly make my job a lot easier."

Carly glared at him before standing on tiptoe to look through the peephole on the door. "It's Rusty."

"The nut from next door?"

"My *friend* from next door," she said, combing her fingers through her wet hair.

Jack retrieved his gun from the closet and stuffed it into the waistband of his denim jeans, then he pulled his T-shirt over the protruding handle. "You can let him in," he said, seating himself on the sofa, then propping one foot up on the coffee table.

Carly swiped open the newly installed dead bolt. "Thank you so much for giving your permission," she said between clenched teeth. "I had every intention of letting him in."

A smile tugged at Jack's lips as she threw open the door with a vengeance and the man standing behind it jumped back in fright.

"Rusty, what a nice surprise." Carly stepped into the hallway to pull him inside.

Although the bill of his baseball cap still quivered, the man offered her a tentative smile as he walked into the apartment. His cap rode low over a hairless brow, almost touching the thick, black horn-rimmed glasses that magnified his green eyes. "I hope I'm not bothering you."

"Not at all," Carly chimed. "You're never a bother, Rusty. Come on in and sit down."

Rusty's Adam's apple bobbed at the base of his throat as he watched Carly move into the living room. Then he seemed to remember that he needed to propel his legs forward to walk, and followed her in.

"I know it's early," Rusty began, gripping the clipboard he carried tightly against his chest. The faded green flannel shirt he wore hung almost to his knees, but not quite far enough to hide the small rip in his fatigue pants. "I saw the light under your door and I wanted..." His words trailed off as his glassy gaze focused on Jack. "Oh... you've got company."

"Not really," Carly said, firmly placing her hand under his elbow and propelling him to the armchair.

"The name's Holden," Jack said, half rising off the sofa as he extended one hand.

Rusty curled his fingers around it, his grasp much firmer than Jack expected.

"So, you're Carly's new...roommate?" Rusty intoned, turning to seat himself in the armchair. "I heard she had someone living here with her."

"No, that would be Alma," Carly informed him, propping herself on the arm of Rusty's chair. "She's already out job hunting this morning."

Jack sat forward on the sofa, propping his elbows on his knees. "I'm just here visiting my cousin Carly for a few days before I head on up to Anchorage."

"Alaska?" Rusty asked, his expression skeptical. "Are there a lot of cowboys in Alaska?"

Jack nodded. "There sure are. The cattle industry is thriving."

"Don't forget your dogs," Carly reminded him.

"Oh, right." Jack smiled. "Got my team up there. Champion malamutes. They make a great sled dog."

"Perhaps you'd better cut your visit here a little short, Cousin Jack," Carly said sweetly. "It's the coldest time of the year now, and your poor malamutes must be freezing. You could light a fire to keep them warm." Her voice thickened. "You're so good at that."

Then she turned to Rusty and smiled. "May I get you something? How about a cup of tea?"

"No, thank you." A bright-red flush crept up his neck. "I just came by to circulate this petition. I'd be honored if you'd be the first one to sign it."

"A petition?" she asked curiously, taking the clipboard out of his hands. A stubby pencil rolled off the surface and fell next to Rusty's scuffed combat boots. He reached down and picked it up off the floor. Then he offered it to her, like a sacrifice to a goddess.

"This is a petition to repair the elevator," Carly said as she scanned the paper attached to the clipboard.

Rusty nodded, craning his neck to read along with her. "It's become too unreliable. A death trap, if you will. The tenants of this building shouldn't stand for it any longer. I've written letters to the superintendent and the owner, but they've both been ignored." His hands tightened around his knees. "Now it's time to take more drastic action."

Jack wondered how long this guy had been living across the hall. The man practically drooled every time he looked at Carly. Of course, she didn't help matters by parading in front of him in her bathrobe, all soft and disheveled and alluring. Jack bit down on his tongue to keep from ordering her into her bedroom to put on some clothes.

Carly smiled as she handed him the clipboard. "Thank you, Rusty, for giving me the first opportunity to sign it. But the elevator doesn't really bother me."

"But you got stuck in there," Rusty countered.

Her hand rested gently on his forearm. "I can take care of myself. You don't need to worry about me."

Rusty swallowed audibly and stared hard at her hand while his cheeks turned crimson.

"I'll sign it," Jack offered, reaching for the clipboard.

Rusty held it up and out of his reach. "No. This is for residents only." His magnified orbs narrowed to thin slits as he glared at Jack. "You don't live here."

"I use the elevator," Jack rejoined.

"Well, it doesn't matter anymore," Rusty said,

tearing the petition out of the clipboard. "I've changed my mind."

"Oh, Rusty, don't let me stop you," Carly implored. "If you want to circulate the petition..."

"No," he interjected, shaking his head. "I'd rather not." He ripped the petition in two.

Jack didn't say another word until Rusty left. Then he slowly shook his head. "Wow. And I thought I had strange neighbors."

Carly planted both hands on her hips. "Rusty isn't strange; he's lonely and insecure. You didn't help matters any by glaring at him the whole time."

"If I was glaring, it was at you," he replied. "The next time you entertain, I suggest you put on some clothes. It's hard enough looking for the person threatening you without having to sort through a roomful of panting males to find him."

"I beg your pardon?"

Jack cleared his throat. He didn't sound like a professional bodyguard. He sounded like a boyfriend. A jealous boyfriend. A raving, jealous boyfriend.

He didn't like arguments he couldn't win. He didn't like jealousy either, a newfound emotion that absolutely horrified him. And he definitely didn't like Rusty. If he wanted to do his job—if he wanted to protect Carly from Rusty and all the other paranoid lunatics out there—he needed her on his side.

"I'm sorry you're still upset about last night," he said in the way of a halfhearted apology. "If it makes you feel any better, I did try to smooth things over with Sidra." Carly rolled her eyes. "Threatening to have her arrested on a drunk and disorderly charge is not my idea of appeasing the client."

"Look on the bright side," he said, more than ready to declare a truce. "After everything that happened last night, our next catering job will seem like child's play."

⁂ 4 ⁂

"Don't move," screeched the wiry five-year-old as he advanced on Carly.

She backed into the corner of the well-appointed living room, her eyes glued to the weapon in his hand. Her lungs fought against the iron grip of a panic attack, each breath a struggle. As her heart galloped against her rib cage, she grappled to stay in control. *Get a grip, Weiss.*

"I want hot dogs for my birthday party," demanded Bobby Joe Hodges. He stood waist-level to Carly, dressed in dark pants, plaid suspenders, and a monogrammed green shirt that matched his narrowed green eyes. "The real long ones with lots of ketchup and mustard. And some greasy French fries and lots of onion rings."

Licking her dry lips, she said, "Put that thing away first, Bobby. Then we'll talk."

"No!" he shouted, taking a menacing step toward her. A circle of preschoolers surrounded them, snickering and pointing at Carly.

"I don't want tofu," Bobby exclaimed, his pink cheeks turning fire engine red. "I won't eat tofu. *I hate tofu*!"

Carly forced her eyes away from the object in his hand and tried to speak calmly. "Your mommy and daddy really wanted you to have tofu. In fact, they insisted. But how about tofu hot dogs? It will just take me a moment to mold them into shape. Add some ketchup and mustard, maybe even throw in a couple of dill pickles..."

"No... no... no!" cried Bobby Joe Hodges, stomping his feet on the floor.

As she suffered through his tantrum, Carly wondered if her Dial-a-Dinner Contest was such a great idea after all. She certainly never envisioned catering a children's birthday party. It would take years before Bobby Joe or his bed-wetting friends could afford to hire her services. And his parents didn't stick around long enough to be impressed by her culinary skills, either. They lit out of here shortly after the cleaning woman escorted her and Jack through the foyer. No doubt their son terrified them as well.

At least Jack was still in the kitchen where he belonged. The last thing she needed was for him to barge in here and rescue her from this thumb-sucking villain. She could handle the situation without that cowboy's help. Any situation. Although she'd relish his gun in her hands right about now.

"So, you want hot dogs?" Carly said, trying to keep her voice calm. A wasted effort since it had to be obvious, even to this group of preschoolers, that she was attempting to claw her way through to the other side of the wall.

"I want a magician, too," demanded the birthday boy, now with visions of grandeur. "Not a stupid clown magician, either. I want a real magician that can make things disappear and that can saw a girl in half." He turned with an evil smile to the little girl with blond pigtails that stood next to him. "I want to see lots of blood."

Great. Another Chester Frey in the making. Only at this moment she'd almost rather face that psychotic than fight off the fiend in front of her. The anonymous note she'd found in her mailbox this morning, with its cryptic verse, didn't frighten her half as much as Bobby and that thing clasped in his grubby little hand.

He suddenly thrust it toward her. Carly turned her head away, unleashing the small scream tethered in the back of her throat.

Jack burst through the kitchen doorway and raced into the living room. "What the..." His words trailed off as he stopped short and blinked at the scene in front of him.

"I... can handle... this," Carly stammered. "Go... back in the kitchen and dish... up the granola."

For a man who thrived on giving orders, he certainly didn't follow them very well. Instead of returning to the kitchen, he leaned against the wall, folded his arms across his broad chest, and grinned at her. She despised him at that moment. Along with her three older brothers, who were to blame for her present predicament. They were the ones who put that rat between her bedsheets all those years ago. They were the ones who still laughed when recalling her hysterics after the lights went out. They were the ones who called it suitable retaliation for a tattling ten-year-old sister. She called it macho revenge. No one knew the incident had left her with a permanent, paralyzing fear of the loathsome rodents.

Until now.

Carly gathered her mounting anger to stare down Bobby Joe. "Get... that... thing... away... from... me," she said between clenched teeth. The sight of his pet rat's twitching pink nose and sharp glistening fangs repelled her as she burrowed further into the corner.

"Only if you get rid of those stupid party hats," he blustered. "I don't want any dumb balloons, either. I'm five now, not a baby."

Catering a birthday party for a group of little kids might not be the job of her dreams but being blackmailed by a five-year-old was positively degrading. Especially with Jack Holden smirking at her from across the room.

Carly took another deep breath and tried not to look at the humpbacked rodent thrust in her face. She needed to extricate herself from this furry situation before she passed out from hyperventilation.

In some unfettered region of her brain, she remembered watching a hostage movie on television. Panic never helped. It was the calm, collected voice of reason that finally saved the day. That, and usually several rounds of machine-gun fire. But then television always leaned toward the dramatic. Carly doubted a SWAT team would descend on this affluent Pine City suburb even if she could get to her cell phone. The only thing between her and it was a big, disgusting rat, hanging from the hand of her latest client.

"Anybody else want anything?" Bobby Joe Hodges

bellowed to his friends. “Cookies? Ice cream? Video games?”

While Bobby basked in the astonished and admiring glances of his peers, Carly looked for an escape route. If she could just make it past the armoire and around the sofa...

“Root beer,” Bobby demanded, his chest swelling with his newfound power. “A big bottle of root beer for everybody.”

The rat squealed as it struggled to escape Bobby’s grasp. Carly closed her eyes and waited to die.

“Hey, Hodges,” intoned Jack’s cool, deep voice. “You ever seen one of these before?”

Carly unscrewed one eye to see him flip open his black leather wallet and reveal a shiny silver badge.

Bobby Joe Hodges Ill’s bravado slipped a trifle. “Yeah. So what? You’re just a waiter. You’re not a sheriff... are you?”

“Worse,” Jack replied tautly, snapping the wallet shut. “I’m a special agent of the state of Texas, working undercover.” He advanced one step, his arms at his sides like a cowboy ready to draw. “It’s my job to protect Ms. Weiss.”

“So?” Bobby Joe Hodges asked, still defiant. “You’re not the boss of me.”

“Looks to me like you might be breaking some laws.”

One of the little girls started to giggle.

"No, I'm not!" countered the little terrorist, then he lowered the rat in his hand. "What laws?"

Jack rubbed one hand over the dark whiskers on his chin. "Let's see now... root beer blackmail... inciting a kiddie riot... carrying a furry weapon."

Bobby narrowed his eyes. "My daddy won't let you take me to jail. He's got lots of money."

"And it's his birthday!" gasped a little girl. "You can't arrest him on his birthday."

"You're right," Jack said with a sigh. "That would make me a party-pooper." He looked over at Bobby. "Maybe if you put your pet rat back in its cage and start acting like a good little citizen of the state of Texas, I might consider droppin' the charges."

With a shout of joyful relief, Bobby fled from the room, rat in hand, as fast as his designer sneakers would carry him.

Carly let out her pent-up breath, her legs barely supporting her weight. She took a faltering step and would've landed smack on the hardwood floor if Jack hadn't caught her up in his arms.

"I could've handled it," she muttered, clinging to him with every ounce of strength she had left.

"You're all right now," he whispered into her hair. "Don't be scared."

"I'm not scared," Carly countered automatically.

She took a deep gulp of air as tremors overtook her body. "I'm just a little shaky from that second cup of coffee I drank this morning."

"Right," he said softly, "nothing scares you. You're perfectly capable of taking care of yourself."

She wanted to wipe that smug smile from his face. Instead, she leaned into the cocoon of his arms. Her heart beat so rapidly in her chest that she was certain Jack could feel it pound through the thin fabric of her blouse.

"Relax now," he ordered gently. "I'll take care of you." He turned his head to the roomful of silent, staring children. "Your lunch is on the table, kids. I give piggyback rides to anybody who cleans their plate." They whooped with delight as they ran down the hallway and into the dining room.

Once they were alone, Jack began to gently knead her taut shoulders. "Relax, Carly."

"Where did you get that badge?" she asked him, closing her eyes at his touch. "You're not really a cop, are you?"

"No," he said with a chuckle. "But my Grandpa Henry worked as a Pine City police officer while I was growing up, along with running Elk Creek Ranch. I used to shine his badge for him, so Grandma Hattie gave it to me after he passed away. I've kept it with me ever since."

Something in his voice made her lean into him. "You must think I'm a wimp," she said, her face buried in his shoulder and her hands locked on his solid forearms.

"I think you're brave and brazen and beautiful."

She looked up at him. "Now you're making fun of me."

"No, I'm not," he replied huskily. He drew her nearer to him, his long fingers caressing the nape of her neck. "I'm comforting you."

A delicious shiver shot down her spine at his touch. Startled by her reaction to his arms around her, Carly closed her eyes, languishing in the sanctuary of his embrace, telling herself she just needed these few moments to regain her composure.

Jack's lips brushed against the part in her hair and then fell to her temple. His fingers gently tangled in her curls as he pulled her head back just far enough to allow his lips to move across her cheekbone and down the length of her jaw. Each sensuous nibble warmed her blood. At last, he found her mouth, and kissed her as a low groan rumbled in the back of his throat.

The adrenaline that had fueled her fear now ignited her passion. She wrapped her arms around his broad shoulders and kissed him with a frantic intensity. His hands slid down her back and rounded her waist. Everything faded to a distant blur... the chatter of children in the next room, the chime of the Waterford clock... the rat. There was only Jack.

"Carly," he groaned softly as he tilted her head back even farther to trail burning kisses down her throat.

"Don't stop," she murmured, burying her fingers in his hair and inhaling its soapy scent.

His arms tightened around her as he deepened the kiss, and she savored every moment of it.

"What kind of business is this?" demanded a shrill voice from the front doorway.

Carly gasped as Jack's lips abandoned hers. He gently unclasped her arms from around his neck as she emerged from her passion-induced euphoria to face unwelcome reality. The parents of that snobby terrorist, Bobby Joe Hodges, stood gaping before them in disbelief.

"Looks like monkey business to me," Mr. Hodges asserted.

"I thought you were caterers," Mrs. Hodges cried, "not exhibitionists! Where are the children?"

Jack ran one finger around the collar of his white dress shirt. "They're in the dining room, enjoying that delicious party food you ordered."

"Momma!" Bobby Joe shot into the living room and hurled himself into his mother's arms. "He...

he…" Bobby Joe stabbed one finger toward Jack, his cheeks bright red. "He wanted to arrest me!"

Carly smoothed down her hair and tried to salvage the situation. "We're all just about to enjoy a wonderful carrot cake with alfalfa sprout frosting. Are you ready to blow out your candles, Bobby Joe?"

Bobby Joe's reply was an angry howl. He flung his arms around his mother's neck. "Make him go away right now!"

Mrs. Hodges cradled Bobby Joe against her and glared in horror at Carly and Jack. "What have you done to my angel?"

"Lady, that kid is no angel," Jack scoffed.

"Jack…" Carly placed a restraining hand on his arm.

"Let me handle this," he said briskly, stepping in front of her to confront the Hodges. "Your son is…"

"So energetic," Carly burst in, peering over Jack's broad shoulder. She moved to his side, trying to subdue her heavy breathing. "I brought along some games if…"

"We've already seen a sample of the games you play, Ms. Weiss," Mrs. Hodges interjected with all the fierceness of a lioness protecting her cub. Then her leonine gaze preyed on Jack. "I'm calling up that radio station right now to demand an apology, on the air, for this travesty they call a prize." Striding past them with her nose in the air, she carried Bobby Joe out of the room.

"And you can forget about catering that business luncheon we talked about," Mr. Hodges added, his derisive gaze roaming intimately over Carly's body. "I don't require the type of service you obviously provide, Ms. Weiss."

Before Carly even had time to form a professional reply to his unflattering complaint, Jack did it for her —with a swift, knuckle-cracking jab to the center of Mr. Hodges cleft chin.

"I shouldn't have let that happen," Jack said, his voice gruff with regret, as Carly drove them over the rain-slickened streets of Pine City.

Words of recrimination and rebuke battled on the tip of her tongue. Words she planned to clobber him with as soon as she started speaking to him again. Not that anything she said would penetrate that thick, cowboy skull of his. Men like Jack and her brothers didn't listen to reason. They didn't respect her right to stand up for herself, either. Jack proved that when he knocked Mr. Hodges on the seat of his custom-tailored trousers.

"There's no excuse for it," he muttered. "I never lose control like that."

The soothing rhythm of the windshield wipers moving over the glass helped ease Carly's frazzled nerves. At least he was suffering remorse for the assault. An unusual emotion for a member of the testosterone club. Most of the time they hit first and boasted about it over a beer later.

Relaxing her murderous grip on the steering wheel, she chalked up the afternoon as just another catering disaster. Raging at Jack for belting one of her customers wouldn't repair the damage. Neither would sending Bobby Joe Hodges a hungry cat as a belated birthday gift.

A hot blush prickled her cheeks as she envisioned herself backed against the wall by a five-year-old. And that turned out to be the high point of the afternoon. Unless she counted those brief, incendiary moments in Jack's arms.

His arms. Her body ached at the memory. A frustrated sigh escaped her lips, still slightly swollen from his kiss. Despite his other faults, the man definitely knew how to kiss. He'd even surpassed the few fantasies she'd allowed herself since first meeting him in the district attorney's office two weeks ago.

But his smothering overprotectiveness and rigid rules were all too real. Jack was bad for her. Just like those wild roots she'd found years ago in North Bend. They look delicious, but you bake them in a quiche and everybody around you starts to double over and turn green around the gills.

Jack's arms might be tempting, but they were even more dangerous. They were a trap, she told herself firmly. Surrendering to him just wouldn't be worth the risk of losing her independence. And she'd come much too far, three hundred miles to be exact, and worked much too hard to give up her autonomy now. No matter what the man could do with his tongue.

"It won't happen again," Jack vowed, rubbing his knuckles. "I promise."

"Don't worry about it," she said, pulling up to a stop sign. "Let's just put it behind us."

He turned to look at her, grim determination steeling his gaze. "You're absolutely right. We both know that kiss was a mistake. A huge mistake. Let's just forget all about it."

A mistake. It took her a moment to speak. "You're apologizing for kissing me?"

Jack raked one hand through his black hair. "We both got carried away. I knew you needed comforting..."

"How dare you!" Carly cried, the tires screeching as she pulled out onto the main thoroughfare. "For your information, I didn't need comforting or rescuing or kissing. A *mistake*," she drawled, "that you initiated."

"Carly, you know my rule about..."

"I do deserve an apology," she continued, cutting off his lame excuse. "In fact, I demand an apology. But not for one innocent, meaningless, entirely forgettable kiss." How could she possibly be attracted to a man as bullheaded as Jack Holden? A man who *apologized* for the most primal, untamed, scorching kiss she'd ever experienced.

The flash of red lights in her rearview mirror drew her attention away from his reply. "Great," she muttered under her breath. "Just what I need—one of Pine City's finest anxious to protect and serve me."

"Pull over," Jack commanded.

Carly glared at him as she tapped on the brake. "What do you think I'm planning to do? Make a run for it? Go on the lam?"

"Possibly. I never know what you're going to do." His chiseled face looked haggard in the glare of the flashing red lights. "And please don't try to wheedle your way out of it by offering to make the officer buttermilk biscuits or sweet potato pie," Jack said as the uniformed policeman approached the driver's side of the vehicle. "Bribery is against the law."

"I don't need to resort to bribery," Carly retorted,

rolling down her window. She smiled brightly at the policeman and extended her hand. "Hi. I'm Carly Weiss."

He looked down at it and said, "May I see your driver's license, ma'am?"

"Of course," she replied, reaching into her purse for her license. "I'm a good friend of Monica Boyle, the district attorney. And this," she said, motioning to Jack, "is my bodyguard. I'm certain he can help clear up any misunderstanding."

"And this is a traffic citation," the officer said, holding up a ticket, "not a misunderstanding."

"For what?" Carly inquired. "I wasn't speeding. In fact, I was driving five miles below the speed limit. I should get extra credit for that." She ignored Jack's snort of amusement.

"Failure to obey a stop sign," the officer explained, reaching for her car registration.

Carly's mouth fell open. "I stopped!" She looked at Jack. "You saw me stop."

Jack shook his head. "You rolled."

Carly urged him with widened eyes to corroborate her story. "You mean I rolled to a stop. Tell the officer that so we don't miss our court date." She turned back to the policeman. "My testimony is vital to the case."

"Your court date's not for two more weeks, Ms.

Weiss," chimed the policeman with a knowing grin. He handed Carly the citation. "Next time, make sure you come to a complete stop before you proceed into the intersection."

She waited until the officer drove off before she shifted the car into gear and pulled away from the curb. "Thanks for all your help," she said wryly. "That cop just issued me a ticket I can't afford to pay. Now I really will have to go on the lam."

"You break the rules, you pay the consequences."

"Me?" Carly's mouth dropped open. "What about you? What about one of the cardinal rules of catering —Thou shall not assault the customer?"

"Hodges had it coming," Jack said shortly. "He crossed the line. He knew it, too. As soon as the words left his mouth." The hand resting on his knee curled into a fist. "There are some unwritten rules. One of them is how you talk to a lady. Hodges broke it."

"And paid the consequence," Carly said, finishing her bodyguard's mantra. "Unfortunately, he won't be paying me for any catering jobs now."

"You're blaming me for that?" Jack asked in amazement. "He wasn't exactly singing your praises before I punched him."

"So you thought a good right hook might convert him?" She shook her head in exasperation. "Your customer service approach needs some fine-tuning. Perhaps in your line of work fists are a tool of the trade. Catering, however, requires a certain finesse."

"Just don't try to finesse me into feeling guilty." Jack shifted in his seat. "That kiss they witnessed is what started all the trouble."

"Trouble is right," Carly muttered to herself as she turned into the Sagebrush Apartments parking lot. She didn't even notice the man standing bare-chested in front of the building until she heard him bellow a familiar name.

"Alma! Alma, sweetheart!" The rain, now a steady downpour, plastered his shaggy blond hair to his head and darkened the thick mat across his chest.

"Let me guess," Jack said as he and Carly hurried across the wet gravel lot. "That's Stanley and this is an off, off, off Broadway production of a Tennessee Williams play."

The heavy rain penetrated her thin cotton blouse and soaked her to the skin. She quickened her steps, resisting the annoying desire to press even closer against Jack's warm body.

"Stay close to me," he ordered, lengthening his stride.

"I'm trying," she said breathlessly, making a mental note to start working out more. She looked up longingly at her dry apartment. Just in time to see

Alma throw open the sixth-floor window and stick her head out.

"Get lost, Stanley," Alma shouted, winging a crystal vase at him. "I'm not your sweetheart. Her name is Gigi, and you found her at that pancakes website, remember?"

Stanley bobbed out of the way as the vase smashed against the wet concrete. Then he stumbled to his knees in the soggy grass. "Alm-ahhh!"

Mrs. Kolinski's white poodle peered through the metal grate of the fire escape on the second floor and began to howl. Stanley dropped his head back and crooned his wife's name again. The poodle joined in two-part harmony.

"I think he's drunk," Carly said when they reached Alma's husband. Whiskey fumes floated from his gaping mouth.

"It's time to go, pal," Jack said, grabbing Stanley by both meaty shoulders and pulling him upright. "Why don't I call you a taxi?"

Stanley wavered on his feet. "I don't want a taxi. I just want my Alma."

"Where's your shirt, Stanley?" Carly asked.

He turned unfocused, bloodshot eyes toward her. "I don't know. I left it somewhere. Alma likes it when I take my shirt off."

"My guess is that he left it in the whiskey bottle

he swam in," Jack said. "He's so zonked, he could be charged with standing while intoxicated."

"I'm drunk with love," Stanley slurred. "I just want my baby back. My Alma." He peered up toward the open window once more and shouted, "Alma! Alm-ahhh!"

"It's over, Stanley," Alma screeched from the open window. She threw a blue gingham pillow down at him. "Cry into that if you feel lonely, you big, dumb jerk!"

The pillow bounced off the top of his head and landed in the mud. Stanley fell to his knees once again at the impact. "Alm-ahhh!"

Carly daintily picked up her sofa pillow by one unsullied corner. At this rate, most of her apartment furnishings would be littering the front lawn before sundown.

She motioned for Jack to follow her. "Let's take him upstairs. He'll drown if we leave him out here with his mouth open."

With an irritated groan, Jack pulled Stanley to his feet. "Come on, big guy," he said as Stanley weaved and wobbled in the rain, finally collapsing against Carly, his beefy hands pawing her arms and shoulders. Jack cursed under his breath and tore Stanley off her before hoisting him up over his shoulder.

"I'm gonna be sick," Stanley moaned, his head

bobbing upside down as Jack carried him into the building.

"Just try it, pal, and I'll shoot you," Jack replied, following Carly down the hallway.

The elevator ride put Stanley to sleep. He sat snoring loudly in the corner until they reached the sixth floor.

"If these doors don't open, I'm petitioning to have this building condemned," Jack said, hitting the control panel with his open palm.

"You're not doing it right," Carly said, punching the doors with her fist, waiting a few moments, and then punching them again. A glow of satisfaction warmed her as the doors slid open with a reluctant whine.

"Next time we take the stairs," Jack muttered, rousing Stanley before dragging him out of the elevator and down the hallway.

"We can't," Carly called after him. "The door jams."

"Doesn't anything in this place work?" he grumbled, steering a wobbly Stanley through her apartment door.

"If you're referring to me," Alma said crisply, "I just applied today at the Sweetshop Candy Factory. They need a nut girl."

Jack opened his mouth just as Carly clapped her hand over it. "Don't say it," she warned him softly.

Alma seemed oblivious to both of them. She was too busy scowling at Stanley. "What's he doing up here? I'm not in the mood for a reconciliation."

"I doubt your husband can even pronounce the word *reconciliation*," Jack said, plopping his cargo down on the armchair, "much less initiate one in the condition he's in. The sooner you fill him full of coffee, the sooner we can call him a cab."

Stanley slowly stood up. "I won't stay where I'm not wanted." He rocked on his feet like a man aboard a ship on a stormy sea. After taking three treacherous steps, he collapsed next to the potted palm. "Don't worry, Alma," he slurred, wrapping his arms around the wide rim of the blue plastic planter, "I'm all right."

Carly's own knees went weak as Stanley's face hovered close to the thick fronds of the palm plant. Much too close for comfort. She made a mental note to avoid using houseplants as hiding places in the future. She needed to stick to places Jack would never look, like in her bed or her bra.

Hoping to create a diversion, she hurried to the other side of the room to rub her hands above the radiator. "There's no heat," she said in an unnaturally loud voice.

"That's because it's ninety degrees outside." Jack tried not to stare at her. Even soaking wet she was gorgeous. Her chestnut hair spilled around her face and curled in damp tendrils down her back. The rain-soaked white blouse and black pants she wore clung to her skin, revealing every silken curve of her body.

"I know, but I'm chilled from the rain," she said with a nervous glance at Stanley, who still hovered over the planter. "Can you fix it? Please?"

For a brief moment, Jack envisioned himself wrapping his arms around her, sheathing her in his warmth. But he'd given in to that fantasy once already today. An error in judgment he didn't intend to repeat. He rolled up his wet shirt sleeves as he moved toward her, hoping some menial work would wipe away the memory of how well her luscious curves molded against him.

"What's this?" Stanley garbled from the corner.

Jack turned away from the radiator to see him pull a slim envelope from the tangle of thick palm branches.

His gut twisted when he realized where he'd seen that color of lavender paper before.

"I wondered what happened to that," Carly said a little too brightly as she hurried across the room.

Alma snatched the envelope out of Stanley's hand. "Who'd put a letter in a plant?"

"Good question," Jack said, grabbing it from Alma before Carly could reach for it. He lifted the torn flap of the envelope and pulled out the single sheet of lavender stationery inside. Eight years on the job and he'd never met a client who took a threat to her life so lightly. Carly Weiss didn't belong in protective custody. She belonged in a mental institution.

"I want some answers," he demanded. "Immediately."

"But I'm soaking wet!" Carly exclaimed, her teeth chattering. "Let me get changed first and then I can explain this little... mix-up."

Jack shook his head, refusing to let her con him into a delay. "I thought it was odd that you'd never received any more threats. Most nutcases, even the harmless ones, can't stop at just one."

"Maybe my nutcase has a lot of willpower," Carly retorted.

"Or maybe you've been deceiving me from the very start. This note is identical to the first one. Same stationery. Same block print. Same death threat."

"But this one rhymes a little better," Carly quipped, reading the note aloud:

"NEVER TRY TO TELL A LIE,
WHEN WE KNOW IT ISN'T TRUE?

OR YOU'LL FIND OUT THE HARD WAY HOW TO TURN A CATERER BLUE."

"Do you know what this means?" he asked, waving the envelope under her nose.

"Honesty is the best policy?"

"It means this person knows your address. He knows where you live!" Jack was angry enough to strangle her himself. "Anything else you're hiding from me? Texts? Emails? Skywriting?"

Carly tilted her chin in the air. "Just one more anonymous note and a piece of blueberry cheesecake. Rusty's never tasted cheesecake. I wanted to save some for him before you stole any more of it." She planted her hands on her hips. "I caught you in the act, Holden, so don't try to deny it, or claim you were pilfering through my refrigerator last night in search of clues."

Jack set his teeth on edge. "This is unbelievable. Some guy threatens to kill you, and you're upset because I sampled some dessert."

"*Some* dessert?" she replied. "The only one who will be turning blue around here is you, judging from the number of blueberries you devoured. Does the word *moderation* mean anything to you?"

He nodded. "As a matter of fact, it does. I'm practicing tremendous moderation at this very moment. Consider yourself lucky."

"Is that a threat, Jack?" Carly asked, drawing herself up to her full five feet, six inches.

Jack rubbed at the sharp pain in his temple. Carly Weiss wouldn't recognize a threat if it came up and bit her on her nicely curved derriere. He closed his eyes to keep from noticing again how that derriere and some other mesmerizing portions of her anatomy were so clearly defined by her saturated clothing.

Another anonymous note.

That would make two more notes she'd received since he moved in with her. And she'd never said a word. The unwelcome thought occurred to him that, perhaps, if he'd spent less time concentrating on Carly's figure and more time figuring out this case, he might have discovered her deception sooner.

He opened his eyes and said coolly, "Of course it's not a threat. I'm a professional, Carly. I don't make threats unless I intend to carry them out."

She shivered beneath his gaze and Jack felt a momentary twinge of regret at his harsh tone. "I'm not trying to scare you..." he began.

"I'm not scared, I'm cold!" Carly interjected. "What's the point of protecting me from a repressed rhymer if I die of hypothermia in the middle of my living room?"

"I want to see that other note," he said briskly.

She pressed her lips into a thin, mutinous line and then spun on her heel and headed toward her bedroom. After what seemed an interminable amount of time, she finally emerged. Her wet clothes had been replaced by a thick terry cloth bathrobe and her hair had been toweled dry so that it hung damply fluffed around her face.

She pulled the note out of the pocket of her robe and handed it to Jack without a word.

He scanned the paper quickly, looking for any clue that might reveal the identity of the author.

ONE, TWO, THREE, FOUR,
SOMEONE'S KNOCKING AT THE DOOR.
FIVE, SIX, SEVEN, EIGHT,
DEATH AND CARLY HAVE A DATE.

"New rules," he bit out. At least he could exercise some damage control. *What if he'd found these notes after losing her to this lunatic? Too late to save her.* "I'll open all the mail from now on. You're obviously not to be trusted. And the door stays locked, twenty-four hours a day. I don't care if Rusty is dying of starvation out in the hallway. You're not to even peer through the peephole without my permission."

Carly groaned. "No more rules. I'll admit that I should have given you these letters sooner. But I didn't believe they'd help, and I honestly thought they might hurt—my business, I mean."

"Perhaps your business is the only way to get through to you." Jack clipped. "If I find out you've hidden any more evidence from me, I'll break your deal with the D.A."

Carly's indigo eyes widened in disbelief.

"That means she'll have to find somebody else, *pay* somebody else," he told her, "to cater that election fundraiser she promised you."

"You can't do that to me!"

"I can and I will," he said, confident that he'd finally made an impression on her. "I told you I don't make threats unless I intend to carry them out. You break the rules, you face the consequences."

Stanley moaned as he lay sprawled out on the hardwood floor. "That's no way to romance her." He hiccupped and the pungent odor of fermentation filled the air. "Don't you know about *The Top Ten Traits of True Love*?"

They both ignored him.

"You're acting as if I'm the bad guy here," Carly accused Jack.

She was closer to the truth than he wanted to admit. She threatened his professional ethics and his very sanity. Especially when she looked at him with those blue flames flickering in her eyes and that hot flush on her cheeks.

"I just want to do this job that I never asked for in the first place," he said.

"Trait number five," Stanley drawled from the floor. "True love speaks with a gentle, caressing tongue."

"Shut up, Stanley," Jack ordered, carefully placing each lavender letter in a separate plastic bag before sealing them shut.

Alma bristled. "There's no reason to take your frustration out on Stanley. He's not the one sending those letters. Carly's not to blame, either just because you can't solve this case. If you're feeling impotent, why don't you find somebody who can help you?"

Impotent. For the first time in his entire life, Jack briefly considered the benefits of that condition.

Then he realized what he was thinking. The horror of it jarred him into action. "That's exactly what I intend to do."

5

Professor Chester Frey bore a remarkable resemblance to the cream puff held in evidence against him. Nearing sixty, the accused murderer had the soft, puffy physique of a man unfamiliar with physical labor.

Jack watched the accused double-murderer lumber into the visitors' room of the county jail. Suddenly he realized why Monica was so nervous about getting a conviction. The mild-mannered professor didn't look capable of handling a slingshot, much less a gun.

"Good afternoon, sir," Professor Frey said, removing his silver-rimmed reading glasses. Small, mud-brown eyes appraised Jack from across the heavily scratched walnut table. "A pleasure to meet you. I assume you're here for a consultation."

"A consultation?" Jack echoed, noting how strange the academic looked in his prison orange jumpsuit, even if it was clean, crisp, and neatly pressed.

"A Love Session," Professor Frey replied, blinking up at him. "Please don't be embarrassed, Mr...." His brow crinkled. "Forgive me, but I've forgotten your name. There have been so many..."

"Holden," Jack interjected. "And I'm not here for a Love Session."

The professor waved away his denial. "Let's not waste time with that sort of nonsense. We both know the reason for your visit. The opportunity for a private session with the creator of *The Top Ten Traits of True Love* is, after all, irresistible. Now, tell me, Mr. Holden," he said, pulling a small notepad and a pen from his pocket, "how I can help you?"

"I'm here," Jack began impatiently, "to ask *you* some questions."

"Naturally. Many of Pine City's finest people meet with me daily for the very same reason. Believe it or not, I first looked upon the invitation to spend time here as an extended sabbatical. Peace. Quiet. Time to reflect upon life and the complex dynamics of interpersonal relationships. Do you know what I found instead?"

"That jail and the Holiday Inn don't have a lot in common?"

The professor shuddered. "That is an understatement. The food served in this institution is most inadequate. As well as the recreational and educational resources. I intend to write a book about these appalling conditions."

"You'll have plenty of time to do it, too," Jack quipped, glancing at his watch.

"I hope so. I've already submitted an outline to my publisher." Frey stroked his grizzled goatee. "But that is a subject for another day. Presently, my hours are filled with requests for romantic advice from the lowliest inmate to the highest public official. And now we're here to talk about you." He twisted open his silver-plated pen, the metal instrument in his hand an odd privilege for a man accused of murder. "Let's begin with your dreams."

"My dreams?" Jack said in surprise.

Frey nodded. "I'm highly qualified to detect sexual symbolism in the unconscious mind. It's amazing how we can cloak our deepest desires in innocuous images."

"I don't have any desires," Jack replied brusquely.

"I see." Frey drummed his short, thick fingers against the tabletop. "So then we're dealing with a case of emotional castration."

Jack opened his mouth to protest the professor's outrageous assumption, then closed it again. He didn't have the time or inclination to defend this nonsense. He needed information. And he needed it before Carly finished giving her deposition in the district attorney's office. "Tell me about that anonymous note you found."

The professor looked up. "Note? I receive hundreds of letters daily from devoted followers. How can you expect me to remember just one?"

"This is the note you turned over to the D.A.'s office. A poem." He recited it to refresh Frey's memory. "Sugar, spice, and everything nice, go into cookies and cake. Falsehoods, fibs, and outright lies do a sorry caterer make."

Gazing up at the flickering fluorescent light on the ceiling, Professor Frey pursed his lips. "Sorry... I don't seem to be able to recall that one."

Jack sat forward in his chair. "You can't recall the threat against Carly Weiss's life?"

The older man slowly shook his head. "No. My mind's a blank."

Jack totally agreed. Unless Frey's apparent amnesia was a ploy designed to strengthen a possible insanity plea. "You do recall Carly Weiss? The key witness in the case against you? The one who will testify about the ruthless murders you committed."

"I'm innocent," chimed the professor.

"That's what they all say."

"But I do recall seeing Ms. Weiss's photograph in the newspapers. A lovely girl, except for that hair, of course. Such a vivid imagination, too."

"Carly didn't imagine seeing you shoot Sophie Odell and Tobias Cobb, Professor."

Frey's face lit up. "Now I know who you are! You're the young man from Cowboy Confidential assigned to protect the caterer until the trial. One of the guards told me all about it." He leaned back in his chair and folded his hands on top of his protruding belly. "Fascinating."

Jack ground his teeth together. He didn't like the man's inside information. Or his ability to bounce from one subject to another like a psychotic ping-pong ball. "We're not here to talk about me."

Frey nodded with a knowing smile. "Of course. Your interest lies with Ms. Weiss and the threat to her life. Tell me all about it."

"That's what I want you to do, Professor," Jack replied, knowing before he ever arrived for this unorthodox jailhouse interview that his chances for success were slim. Still, Frey might let one clue slip, a word or a name that could point Jack in the right direction. "You're the expert on the inner workings of the human mind."

"That's very true."

"You study and understand complex emotions," Jack continued, stoking the older man's ego. "You see things others overlook. People confide in you."

The professor nodded, a smug smile on his lips. "The secrets I could tell you. But, of course, my sources must remain confidential. I have my reputation to consider. Still..."

Jack waited, hope surging unexpectedly within him. Solving this case meant saving Carly. It also meant putting her out of his life before she drove him out of his mind.

"I think I can be of some help to you," Professor Frey said slowly, leaning forward to jot a few notes on his pad.

"Tell me everything," Jack prompted.

A smile wrinkled Frey's puffy features. "Everything? Just how much time do you have, Mr. Holden?"

Jack checked his watch again and realized he should have left five minutes ago. "Just long enough to hear what I need to know."

"Then I'll be brief." Frey lightly tapped the table with the end of his pen. "You're a textbook case, sir. I'm speaking of my textbook of course, *The Top Ten Traits of True Love.* I suggest you study chapter four. It deals specifically with the subject of unrequited love and will give you several practical suggestions for winning Ms. Weiss."

Jack fought down his rising impatience. "I don't want to win her. I'm not in love with her. My only concern is protecting her. That's my job. I don't know how I can make my position any clearer."

Frey chuckled. "You're a prime example of the sexually frustrated male. Irritable... tense... combative. You might find it helpful to also read the romance outline in chapter three."

"As if I'd take romantic advice from a man who solves his problems with a .357 Magnum."

"Sarcasm does not become you, sir," Frey said, obviously affronted. "If that is the way you talk to Ms. Weiss, it is no wonder that she shuns you. Love speaks with a gentle, caressing tongue."

"So I've heard. But I'm not interested in your ten traits, Professor. I'm looking for a suspect. I want the name of the person who wrote that note." Even as he spoke the words, Jack knew Frey himself might be behind the threats. Orchestrating every move from his jail cell. The idea wasn't inconceivable. In fact, it was appallingly easy. A bribed guard, a slew of devoted fans, an analytical, if warped, mind all added up to a dangerous scenario. "One name, Professor. That's all I want."

Frey emitted a wistful sigh. "We don't always get

what we want, Mr. Holden. You'll find that in chapter eleven of my book, under the subtitle, Fads and Fetishes." The professor closed his notepad. "Come back after you've finished my book and we can talk some more. By the way, I'll be more than happy to autograph it for you."

Jack stood up and strode toward the door, now more frustrated than ever. His instincts told him the nutty professor knew something. Or someone. Like the person threatening Carly. Unfortunately, Jack didn't have the time to play the professor's games. He hit the buzzer to signal the guard.

"One last word of advice," Professor Frey called after him. "From chapter nine. It seems particularly suited to your situation, Mr. Holden." He arched a snowy brow. "Never mix business with pleasure unless you're willing to pay the price."

Jack burst into the district attorney's office without bothering to knock. "Where is she?"

Monica Boyle sat behind her massive desk, speaking softly into the telephone receiver. Her serene brown gaze fixed on Jack as he paced across the room. After jotting down a few notes in the file in front of her, she replaced the receiver on the hook. "Please come in, Jack," she said wryly, "and have a seat. I presume you're talking about Carly Weiss?"

"She's not in the deposition room or in the ladies' room or anywhere on this floor," he said, checking his watch for what seemed like the hundredth time since he'd left her.

"I've only been gone thirty minutes and already your office has managed to lose track of her."

"Don't you think you're overreacting just a bit?"

He placed both palms against the smooth mahogany surface of her desk. "I'm tired of everybody telling me I overreact. This woman's life is at risk. She is now missing. I'd like to know how you'll react when tomorrow's headlines read, 'Key Witness Disappears From District Attorney's Office.'"

Monica paled slightly but kept her composure. "Don't even joke about a thing like that."

"I'm not joking. But it sure seems like I'm the only one taking these threats against Carly seriously. Including Carly herself. Did you see those notes I turned over to your office?"

Monica nodded and pulled the file toward her. "That was the lab on the telephone. They didn't find any fingerprints on the paper, other than yours, Carly's, and those of Alma and Stanley Jones." She glanced up at him. "Are you protecting a witness over at the Sagebrush Apartments or throwing a party?"

"Most of the time I'm trying to maintain my sanity." He started pacing across the floor again, plowing his fingers through his thick hair. "But I can handle it, Monica. Don't worry. Now where in the hell is Carly?"

Monica watched him stride back and forth. "Sit down, Jack, you're making me dizzy. She just went for a cup of coffee."

His mouth dropped open. "And you let her go alone?"

"All the way to the second floor," she replied. "I doubt anyone, even a lunatic, would attempt to attack her in the county court building. The halls are full of deputies and other official personnel."

"I'm not worried about a lunatic. I'm worried about Carly. Do you realize how much trouble she can get into in a matter of moments? When she told you she wanted to go for coffee, she probably meant to Brazil! She's got a mind of her own and a will stronger than hot mustard sauce."

The district attorney arched one brow. "Hot mustard sauce?"

"It's a seasoning agent," he said absently, wondering if he should call for a building evacuation to flush Carly out.

"I know what it is, Jack. I've just never heard a witness compared to a condiment before."

"Carly's different," he stated, peering out the window to the street below. *When he got his hands on her...*

"Obviously. Is there something going on here I should know about?"

"Nothing I can't handle," he muttered. Nothing but one kiss, a few stolen glances, and way too many provocative fantasies to allow him a decent night's sleep in over two weeks. But aside from the one very brief, very physical encounter at that birthday party, he'd maintained his professional distance.

"What exactly does that mean?" Monica asked.

"It means that if this cowardly creep doesn't kill her, then I just might. She's the most obstinate, reckless, irresponsible client I've ever encountered. I'm counting the days, no... *the minutes...* until I never have to see her again."

Monica's eyes narrowed. "I assume you've had difficult clients before. What makes Carly so different?"

Jack couldn't even begin to explain. Especially when he didn't understand himself. Her breezy disregard for danger... her oddball assortment of friends... her throaty, irreverent laugh.

"Nothing," he replied shortly. "I've got everything under control."

"I hope so." Monica folded her hands on top of her desk. "Because there's too much at stake in this case to blow it now."

Jack turned away from the window. "I have no intention of blowing anything. I'm a professional..."

The door opened and Jack almost jumped out of his skin. "Where in the hell have you been?" he roared, turning to see Monica's tiny, ancient receptionist quivering in the doorway.

"In... in the ladies' room," the senior citizen stammered. "Stall three. Remember?"

Jack took a deep breath. "Yes, I'm sorry about that, ma'am." Then he helped her into the office before heading for the door.

"Wait a minute, Jack." Monica rose out of her chair, both hands braced on the top of her desk.

"Yes?" he said, stopping in the doorway.

"I know you're frustrated with Carly but be careful. When bodyguards lose their objectivity, they start to make mistakes. Neither one of us can afford any mistakes in this case."

Jack replied with a brief nod and then headed for the elevator. He didn't tell her about the mistake he'd already made. The mistake that still shook him to his core when he thought of Carly pressed against him, her mouth soft and hot on his. He'd almost broken his most rigid rule. He'd almost trashed his credibility as a bodyguard for a woman who broke every rule in the book just to get what she wanted.

No more. No more compromises, either. With only a week left before the trial, he'd lay down the law to Carly. His law.

But first, he had to find her.

Carly smiled politely at the man seated at her table in the coffeehouse while her eyes strayed to the large plate glass window. The courthouse loomed across the busy street and Jack was still stalking the side-walk in front of it, looking ready to eviscerate someone with his bare hands.

She smiled. Freedom tasted even better than the chocolate biscotti she'd ordered with her latte. Especially freedom from the man who deeply regretted kissing her.

"We're all set for Friday night," her latest client said, rubbing his hands gleefully together. "I'm so excited I can hardly sit still!"

Carly assumed the three cups of cappuccino Niles

Winsett had downed in the last half an hour had something to do with it. Still, it soothed her caterer's pride to finally have a customer excited about the prospect of her services. Even if the job did sound rather bizarre.

"I know you'll be happy with the menu we've selected," she said before taking a sip of her latte. Her eyes strayed to the window once again. Jack was still out there.

"I'm certain the food will be delicious," Niles replied. "The first of many dinners catered in my home by Carly's Creations." He lifted his cappuccino cup in a toast.

"I'll drink to that," Carly exclaimed as she clinked her cup against his. Progress. At last. Her Dial-a-Dinner idea would finally pay off. Just in time to prevent her rubber checks from bouncing her into bankruptcy.

Niles rose to his feet, wrapping his black cape around his narrow shoulders. "Forgive me, Carly, but I've already stayed too long. I must return home to my darling Marguerite."

"That's perfectly all right," she replied as she watched Jack cross the street and walk past the window. He stopped short when he finally spied her through the glass. Her smile faded as she met his gaze, his gray eyes stormy with indefinable emotions.

The next moment they cleared and shone hard as flint. The concern that had clouded them obviously had been just a figment of her overactive imagination.

Niles sighed wistfully. "My wife and I have so little precious time left together. I shouldn't want to waste another moment."

"Thank you so much for meeting me here today, Mr. Winsett," Carly said, distracted by the swish of the front door. A wave of warm air rushed into the cool coffee shop and curled around her legs.

"It's been my pleasure," Niles said and then turned to leave with a dramatic swirl of his long cape.

Carly sensed rather than saw Jack's brawny form approach her table. Her heart began to race, which she blamed on the latte.

"I've been looking for you everywhere," he began, his voice unnaturally calm.

She opened her mouth to explain but he held up one hand to ward her off.

"Who was that guy?" He leaned forward, his palms resting heavily on the round marble table. "And why is he wearing a cape? In August? In Texas?"

"It's a long story," she said, certain he wouldn't like it. "You seem upset."

"Oh, I'm more than upset." He kicked out a chair and sank into it. "Do you have any idea how valuable you are to the state's case against Frey? Without you, that murderer, that crazy egomaniac, could walk the streets a free man."

He waved away the approaching waiter. "There's even more than your life at stake, Carly. There's retribution for the lives of Sophie Odell and Tobias Cobb. There's the safety of the public at the large. If Frey walks, he'll milk his experience for all the publicity it's worth. Is that what you want?"

"What I want never seems to matter. I'm a person, too, Jack. A woman. Not just a walking witness."

"Don't you think I know that?" he said huskily. "I was frantic to find you. I barreled through half the people in the courthouse looking for you. I even startled an old lady when I searched the restrooms."

She pushed her empty latte cup aside. "It's not my fault you overreacted."

"You're right," he conceded. "I'm the one to blame for letting you out of my sight in the first place." He heaved a deep sigh, then leaned toward her. "My imagination ran wild. I just kept hoping I could find you in time, that I could tell you everything I'm feeling for you."

She blinked. Was this Jack Holden talking? The by-the-book bodyguard who ruled her days? The sexy cowboy whose handsome face and sinewy body invaded her dreams at night? The man who suddenly looked more alluring than that slice of chocolate chip cheesecake in the refrigerated display case?

And she'd thought he didn't care.

Carly cupped her chin in her palm and gazed dreamily at him. "Really, Jack?"

He reached across the table for her hand. "Really. You're like no woman I've ever met before. Carly, I..." Anguish flooded his voice as he struggled to get the words out. "I can't go on like this. You've got to start acting like a normal witness. And you have to stop taking so many risks."

Startled by this unexpected display of emotion, she gently laid her hand in his palm. She'd never really looked at his hands before. They were broad, with long fingers that tapered to smooth, blunt cut nails. Powerful enough to subdue an assailant, tender enough to arouse a lover.

He clenched his fingers around her hand, clinging to it. Remorse ran through her. Poor Jack! She'd reduced him to this state. She'd run roughhouse over him without any thought to his feelings. Maybe this was the time to confess her own tumultuous emotions to him.

"Jack, I..." Her words faltered when he slapped a handcuff around her left wrist.

"Gotcha." His gray eyes glowed like burnished steel.

An outraged cry escaped her lips as she struggled against the metal snare.

Jack slipped the other end of the handcuff around his right wrist, impervious to her attempts to escape. "Shall we go now, or would you like another latte?"

"Get this thing off me!" she cried, gaping in disbelief at the solid steel cuff imprisoning her to Jack Holden. All her warm, fuzzy feelings for him faded away at the predatory gleam in his eye.

"I will," he promised. "Right before you're sworn in on the witness stand."

That was seven days from now. And nights. The implications of her predicament took her breath away. It was too ludicrous to be believed. To be tolerated. How dare he treat her like a common criminal!

"You're bluffing," she cried as a fresh spurt of primitive anger burst through her. Carly wriggled the handcuff around her wrist, twisting and pulling, hoping to slip her hand through the small opening. It was impossible.

"Maybe," he said and grinned. Then he stood up and turned toward the door.

She had no choice but to follow him. It was either that or get dragged by her heels through downtown

Pine City. And judging by the implacable expression on his face, he'd be perfectly happy to drag her.

Cars honked and passersby stared as Jack led her across the busy street with their wrists linked together by the cuffs. By the time they reached her parked car, several people walking along the sidewalk had stopped to stare. A group of tourists pointed their cell phones at Carly and Jack and started snapping pictures.

"All right," Carly said, gasping for breath when they reached her car. "You've made your point. Now unlock these cuffs."

"Not until we come to an understanding." He pointed to her windshield. "Do you see that?"

She looked at the sprig of rosemary pinned underneath the windshield wiper. "Really, Jack, you shouldn't have."

"I didn't," he snapped. "Do you know what it means?"

"Yes." She plucked the sprig off the windshield with her free hand, studying the spiky green leaves. "Now I can add fresh rosemary to my roast chicken tonight."

"Rosemary is for remembrance," he told her. "You know—*Violets for faith, daisies for hope, and rosemary for those in heaven above. Lilies bring peace, marjoram joy, and roses are given for love...*" He cleared his throat. "And so on."

"A poet and a bodyguard," Carly drawled, rolling her eyes. "How lucky can a girl get?"

"I'm no poet. Those are just words to a song my mother used to sing." Something flickered over his face. "Anyway"—he pointed to the wilting sprig of rosemary in her hand—"this signifies death. Someone is stalking you, Carly. Someone who likes to play games. Someone who wants to kill you. He's probably watching us right now."

It took all her willpower not to peer around the street for a skulking maniac. Especially now that someone in the gathering crowd had started a freedom chant. Then she looked into Jack's eyes and saw a glimmer of fear there and something else that made her stomach feel funny.

Maybe he had a point. The least she could do was meet him halfway. Reaching into her purse with her free hand, she pulled out her car keys and tossed them to him. "Let's get out of here."

He caught them with his right hand, then led her around to the driver's door. After he opened the door, she scooted inside, awkwardly heaving herself over the console and into the passenger seat. Jack was right beside her, the wrists still cuffed together as he settled into the driver's seat.

"Will you let me go now?" she asked.

Jack shook his head. "First, we're going to have what's called a one-sided conversation. I talk and you listen."

"You're going to pay for this, Jack." She really wanted to hate him. She focused all her energy on hating him. On forgetting that kiss and the haunted look she'd glimpsed in his eyes the moment before he'd spotted her in the coffee shop.

"Maybe. But right now, I'm the one with the key to the handcuffs."

She inched nearer to him on the seat, the skin on her wrist already chafing at the pull of the heavy cuff. The problem was that Jack was so big the front seat of her car seemed cramped in comparison. Almost intimate.

Tilting her chin in the air, Carly said, "I just want you to know that I'm planning to file a complaint with the district attorney's office, the police department, and anyone else who will listen."

"It won't do you any good. They'd all be on my side. So you can either choose to cooperate or get used to me cuffed to your side twenty-four hours a day."

"What do you mean by cooperate?" she asked through clenched teeth.

"First, I want you to get rid of Alma. I can't keep

track of her when she comes and goes at all hours of the day and night. I don't *want* to keep track of her. Or Stanley. I've got enough to worry about without watching the two of them act out the death scene of their marriage."

A pins and needles sensation prickled up Carly's left arm. Jack probably cut off her circulation when he cuffed her. With any luck her blood-deprived hand would shrivel up and drop off in a few days and she'd be free.

"There's also the matter of Rusty."

She waited in resentful silence for him to continue, her face turned toward the passenger window. The crowd was finally beginning to disperse.

"He's totally off-limits to you from now on. I'll pick up his newspaper for you. I'll also deliver his spaetzle."

"Rusty's harmless."

Jack snorted. "I did a little background check on your harmless friend Rusty. He earned a bachelor's degree from SMU five years ago and then became a graduate assistant to none other than Professor Chester Frey."

"I don't believe it," she replied, her wrist now completely numb.

Jack reached into his jacket and pulled out a small spiral notebook, tossing it onto the seat next to her.

"It's all in there. Including the telephone number of my contact at the university. Check it out yourself if you don't believe me."

"No, I mean I can't believe that Rusty graduated from college." She shook her head in wonder. "He never told me that."

Jack shook his head. "I think you missed the punch line, Carly. Rusty worked *very closely* with the now infamous professor. Your neighbor had a close, working, *mentor* relationship with a homicidal genius. Who knows how it affected him? Even you have to admit that Rusty is a little strange."

"He's just shy and sensitive," Carly said coolly.

"Well, from now on we're avoiding sensitive. We're also avoiding kooky which means Alma, and desperate which means Stanley."

"What about Niles Winsett?"

Jack glared at her. "Who is Niles Winsett?"

"The guy with the cape. He just happens to be the third winner of my Dial-a-Dinner contest." Even as she spoke the words, she knew he'd forbid her to cater until after the trial. She'd pushed him too far when she'd disappeared without permission. The bile of bitter defeat rose in her throat. She'd come so close to success. Until Jack Holden *protected* her from it.

"That Dracula impersonator is your next client? What does he want you to cater, a blood drive?"

"Don't be ridiculous," she retorted, deciding now would not be the best time to regale him with the unusual details of the Winsett party. "It's simply a catered dinner scheduled for next Friday evening."

"All right," he said.

"All right?" She wondered if the numbness in her arm had traveled up to her ears. "I can cater for the Winsetts? Do you mean it?"

Jack gave a brief nod. "I told you the day I moved into your apartment that I wouldn't interfere with your Dial-a-Dinner contest. I never break my word."

She smiled her relief, thankful for the first time for one of his precious rules.

"Now," he said, taking a small metal key out of his pocket and holding it up in the air, "do we understand each other?"

Some of Carly's joy faded. It would be impossible to cater anything while she was chained to Jack. And she knew the only way he'd unlock the handcuffs was if she agreed to his ridiculous demands about Alma and Rusty. She looked from the key to the cuffs and back again. A blush warmed her neck when she thought about how easily she'd fallen into his trap. How she'd held his hand. How she'd wanted to hold a lot more than his hand.

The jerk.

"Perfectly," she said, promising herself that she'd make him pay for his underhanded tactics.

"Good. I'm not enjoying this either, Carly. I want our time together to end as much as you do." He inserted the key into the lock. "Maybe more. As soon as it does, I can go back to herding cattle instead of bullheaded clients."

Then he unsnapped the handcuffs and released her.

Carly's pride hurt even more than her wrist. He obviously couldn't wait to be rid of her. As if she were some annoying pest he was forced to keep with him until she gave her testimony at the trial. The fact that she didn't want Jack Holden, or even *like* him very much, didn't appease her one bit.

"Sorry I had to play hardball," he said, pocketing the handcuffs. "You've got nobody to blame but yourself."

"That's so typical," she said hotly, the windows in the car steaming over. "I never asked to witness a murder. I never asked for you, either, if you'll remember. So don't try to pretend like your badass bodyguard routine is doing me any favors."

"Does this mean I shouldn't expect a thank-you note?"

Carly picked up the sprig of rosemary off the car

seat and dropped it into her purse. "Don't worry. I'll find some way to repay you for all you've done for me. Consider yourself warned."

Carly turned toward the window as Jack started the engine, her vision clouded by the red haze in her eyes. He'd pay. Jack Holden would most definitely pay.

6

"You're kicking me out?"

"Think of it as a relocation opportunity," Carly replied, and then held up both hands to ward off Alma's impending hysterics. She was seated on the edge of the double bed, watching Alma apply bleach to the dark roots of her platinum hair in front of the mirror.

That impulsive dye job was proof that Alma didn't take rejection well. Specifically, rejection from men. Which gave Carly ample reason not to tell her the truth about why she was giving her the boot. Divulging that Jack wanted her out of the apartment might drive her friend over the edge.

"There are a lot of great reasons for you to leave," Carly said, trying to ease into the eviction.

"There are a few good reasons for me to stay,"

Alma countered. "Like a roof over my head, indoor plumbing, and the counsel of my best friend. Or should I say former best friend?"

"Don't be silly. Of course, I'm your best friend. Otherwise, I wouldn't ask you to leave."

"That's the dumbest thing I've ever heard you say."

"Think about it," Carly continued. "You've never really been on your own. You lived with your folks until you got married, and then with a husband. It's time to prove your independence. As long as you stay here, with Stanley hovering in the wings, you're like a sky diver afraid to step out of the plane."

"So you've decided to push me?"

"Think of it as an encouraging shove."

Alma lowered the styling wand. "You can't fool me. This is about you and Jack. He's the reason you want me out of here, isn't he, Carly? You want the man all to yourself."

"Don't be ridiculous." Carly plopped on her stomach across the length of the bed, cupping her chin in her palms. "I can barely stand to be in the same room with him."

"Which is why my leaving you two here alone makes such perfect sense," Alma muttered sarcastically. "Give me a break! You and Jack generate so much electricity you don't need to worry about paying your power bill."

"That's a complete exaggeration," Carly retorted, certain the fact that her lights were still working after missing one month's payment had nothing to do with Jack.

"What I *really* can't believe," Alma continued, "is that you'd dump your best friend out onto the streets of Pine City for a man." Her lower lip quivered. "I'd never treat you like that."

Carly's mouth fell open. "What about the time you left me at the Frosty Spoon on Old Highway 62 so you could ride off with Bart Stolz in your convertible? I had to walk ten miles, *in the dark,* to get home."

"That was different."

"Hardly."

"That was in North Bend," Alma retorted. "The walk probably did you good, anyway. You'd eaten a banana split *and* a butterscotch sundae that night, remember? You were worried about fitting into your prom dress, so I figured you needed the exercise."

"Thanks," Carly replied. "Just think of this as my returning the favor. Anyway, you've been complaining about the cramped quarters here and living out of your suitcase. Wouldn't it be nice to have a bathroom all to yourself for a change?"

"I don't know. This place has certain... amenities that I'm not sure I want to give up."

Carly quickly tried to dissuade her of that notion. "Like a temperamental elevator? A scalding shower every morning, courtesy of Mrs. Kolinski? Or maybe the panoramic view of the feedlot just outside of town?"

Alma turned back to the mirror. "You have everything, Carly, and you don't even realize it. Or appreciate it. You get to live in this fun town and meet all kinds of new people." She put the finishing touches of bleach on her bangs. "And just look at your career. You're not even thirty years old yet and you run your own business. You don't even have a college degree."

"What about my diploma from the Cottonwood Cooking Academy?" Carly said. "I graduated with honors."

"From on an online cooking school," Alma said. "Where you learned about sugar, spice, and everything nice. I spent six years earning a master's degree in theater and ended up pressing shirts at Ollie's Dry Cleaners in North Bend while you started your own business. Then you even got to witness a murder! You bounce from one adventure to another."

Carly sat up on the bed. "In case you haven't noticed, my life isn't exactly one big game show. My business is almost bankrupt and someone may be trying to kill me."

"And then there's Jack," Alma continued. "I mean, what is it, Carly, that you've got that I haven't got? We're both young, attractive, and currently available. You barely know the guy and already you're living together!"

"It's not like that, Alma, and you know it."

Alma wiped the bleach off the styling wand with a tissue. "Not yet anyway. You really aren't in love with that cowboy, are you?"

"Of course not."

"Maybe you're just infatuated, or *in lust* with the man. That could explain your confusion."

"I'm not confused," Carly said. "Now what were we talking about before Jack?"

"My independence."

"Right. I think you'll really enjoy it, Alma, once you get used to the idea."

Alma studied her brassy locks in the mirror. "What if you get used to the idea of having Jack around? He's not right for you, Carly. What about common interests? Compatibility? One clue that you two agree on anything besides disagreeing with each other?"

"We're exact opposites," Carly affirmed.

"Well, opposites attract, don't they?" Alma countered. "Even if he is everything you've chafed against your whole life. Cut from the same beefcake cloth as your big brothers. The other day, I actually saw him drink milk out of the carton. Could you live with that?"

"You don't have to convince me, Alma. I know the man is impossible."

"Even if he's the sexiest thing to show up in your life since that male stripper at my bachelorette party?"

Carly waved a hand in airy dismissal. "Don't worry about me. We kissed once and he almost developed laryngitis repeating what a huge mistake we'd made. I'm safe with him in more ways than one."

"Jack kissed you?" Alma's eyes widened. "Where?"

"On the lips."

"That's not what I meant. But I suppose it doesn't matter anyway. The question is, why? I thought you said he has a rule against that sort of thing."

"He does," Carly agreed, although she didn't bother to tell Alma that no rule could've stopped the sparks between them. Passion ignited. Desire sizzled. The tofu almost burned to a crisp on the Hodge's kitchen stove. She mentally shook herself. "And so do I. At least where Jack Holden is concerned. Especially since he handcuffed me."

"He kissed you and handcuffed you?" Astonishment shone in her green eyes. "So much for his wholesome cowboy act." Tightening the belt of her robe, Alma said, "That does it. Now I am definitely staying. I don't think it's safe to leave you here alone with Jack."

"You've got it all wrong," Carly began.

Alma planted her hands on her hips. "I know a lot more about men than you, Carly. I lived with Stanley for an entire year and look what happened to us. I don't want you to come home someday and find Jack having fiber optic sex."

"That's something I'll *never* have to worry about. But Jack really isn't the issue here..."

"Why not? Men are alike. And Stanley is every bit as sexy as Jack." Alma tossed her hair over her shoulder. "He's also crazy in love with me. You should see the beautiful bouquets of flowers he sends me at work. The girls there think I'd be crazy not to go back to him."

Carly looked up in surprise. "I think *crazy* is the key word. Are you actually considering it?"

Alma shrugged. "I'm not sure what to do. On the one hand, Stanley can be charming, funny, and cuddly as a newborn puppy. On the other hand, he drinks too much, ogles every woman in sight, and works only when the mood strikes him." A long, wistful sigh escaped her lips. "I don't know what I want."

"How about your own apartment with a working elevator and enough closet space to hold your collection of Marlon Brando memorabilia?"

"As tempting as that sounds, I'm too good a friend to leave you here alone with that guy." Alma treated her to a patronizing smile. "Let's face it, Carly, your experience with men is severely limited. The guys in North Bend knew better than to mess with the Weiss boys' little sister. But here in Pine City it's a different story. Without your big brothers around, someone has to protect you."

Carly buried her face in the bedspread to smother her scream of frustration. Protect her from what? Heavy breathing? A torrid romance? Wild, steamy passion? Not that she'd ever had any experience with steamy passion, according to Alma. Not that she'd want any involving Jack.

"So, it's all settled," Alma said with a satisfied sigh. "I'm staying."

Carly gave up trying to spare her friend's feelings. "You can't stay, Alma. You don't have any choice in the matter. Jack told me you have to go."

Alma arched a sparsely plucked brow. "Since when do you start taking orders?"

"Since he and I made a deal," Carly explained reluctantly. "My end of it includes helping you pack."

Alma froze, staring in disbelief at Carly's reflection in the mirror. "You're actually choosing that two-hundred-pound hunk over me?"

"I don't look at it that way," Carly said brightly, hoping her enthusiasm might be contagious. "I see it as a chance to let you spread your wings and fly."

"Wouldn't it be a lot easier to just hurl me over a cliff instead?"

"Don't take it personally, Alma; this is really for the best," Carly said, guilt twisting her gut. "Besides, you know you can find a decent apartment—one probably a whole lot nicer than this."

"True," Alma said stiffly. She looked disdainfully around the small bedroom. "This isn't exactly how I pictured life in the fast lane."

"It's the pits," Carly agreed fervently. "A dive. The scourge of Pine City. Don't think of leaving here as moving out but moving up. You told me money isn't a problem. Maybe we could even find you a nice condo."

Alma's face crumpled. "I can't believe you're serious about this. Jack wins and I lose? You really want me out of here?"

Carly sat up and hugged the pillow to herself. "I'm sorry, Alma. I'll help you look for a decent place... pack... even cook up some gazpacho as a house-warming present. I know that's your favorite."

"If you want me to go, I'll go," Alma snapped,

vigorously rubbing night cream onto her face. "Nobody needs to ask me twice. I can leave right now."

Carly winced at her friend's brusque tone. "That's silly. First thing in the morning will be soon enough."

"How generous of you." She slammed the lid back on the jar of night cream. "At least now I know what our friendship means to you. But I promise that after Jack breaks your heart, I'll refrain from saying I told you so. It's your life. If you want to take a chance with some sexy cowboy who's into handcuffs, that's your choice. I won't stand in your way."

"I'm sorry, Alma. I know you'll always be there for me."

"That makes one of us, anyway."

Carly shook her head. "That's not true. Think of this as an adventure. Tomorrow you start down an exciting, uncharted road. I've already contacted a real estate agent to act as your tour guide."

Stomping over to her side of the bed, Alma flung her slippers against the wall before she climbed under the covers.

"Won't that be fun?" Carly asked hopefully.

"I can hardly wait," Alma sniffed. "What other entertainment do you have planned for me? A root canal? Or maybe a nice head-on collision?"

Closing her eyes at the tremor in Alma's voice, she said, "Please don't take this personally."

"Of course not," Alma hissed. "It's not like we're friends or anything."

Carly didn't know what else to say. It didn't matter now anyway because Alma wasn't listening. She'd turned toward the wall and covered her head with a pillow.

She obviously wasn't taking this as well as Carly had hoped. And it was all Jack's fault. Swallowing the lump in her throat, she removed her contact lenses. He couldn't be happy just cramping her independence and punching a catering customer. No. Not Jack Holden. He needed to make certain all her friends despised her as well before he walked out of her life.

To teach her a lesson.

Those weren't his words, of course, but Carly knew the firm hand of domination when she was handcuffed to it.

Fine. She could teach him a few lessons, too. Like, rules were made to be broken. She lay awake in the strained, silent darkness as a plan germinated and took root in her mind. Making Jack break his most sacred rule would do more than teach him a lesson. It would avenge her of that mortifying incident in the coffee shop. And for hurting Alma.

Of course, it would involve kissing Jack again. *Forcing* herself to kiss Jack again. A small price to pay for the satisfaction of looking up into his steely-gray eyes and saying, *Gotcha.*

And she knew the perfect time and place to do it.

The only thing worse than having Jack Holden as her bodyguard was having a *sick* Jack Holden as her bodyguard.

"I think you'll live," Carly told him, peering at the digital thermometer she'd just pulled from his mouth.

"Don't sound so disappointed," he grumbled in a dry, gravelly voice. Tugging the blanket up under his chin, he moaned softly at the exertion. He lay propped up on two plump pillows, a folded, damp washcloth draped over his forehead.

Ever since he'd gotten up this morning, he'd been suffering from body aches and a bad attitude. After dragging himself to the breakfast table and then almost collapsing into his cereal bowl, he'd grudgingly admitted to not feeling well. By noon he'd declared himself ready for the morgue. Carly finally convinced him to lie down instead of calling the coroner.

He looked thoroughly miserable stretched out on her living room sofa, his flushed cheeks stubbly with black whiskers. Crisp, curling black chest hair peeked out from the top of the blanket. His large bare feet hung over the end of the sofa.

She almost felt sorry for him.

Until she remembered that he'd banished Alma to a beautiful penthouse apartment with a view of the Pine City skyline. And taped his long list of rules to Carly's refrigerator door. And handcuffed her in public. She toyed with the idea of taking advantage of the situation to get even with him. But she always fought fair. She'd wait until he was healthy and hardheaded again. Then she'd let him have it.

"Disappointed? Are you kidding? Not when you're this much fun to have around." Carly wiped off the thermometer, then slipped it back in the plastic sleeve. "Besides, I need you alive and well in two days to help me cater the Winsett party."

"I'll be there whether you want me or not," he growled. "Unless I starve to death first."

She smiled. "Didn't that cough syrup fill you up?"

"Cough syrup?" he scoffed. "You mean that turpentine you poured down my throat? I wanted to call the poison control center, but I couldn't reach my phone."

"I think you're getting cranky," she said. "Although it's a little hard to tell." Walking over to the windows, she pulled down the shades. "Why don't you take a nap?"

Jack didn't trust that innocent expression on her face. "So you can sneak out the door while I'm asleep?" He shook his head and then winced at the pain. "Not a chance."

Walking back to his side, Carly laid her soft hand against his prickly cheek. "You couldn't stop me if you wanted to. You're burning up."

He closed his eyes at her tender touch. "Just try and walk out of here, Carly, and you'll see how strong I really am. Nothing stops me from doing my job." He gulped as her fingers began lightly stroking his brow. "Nothing and nobody."

A fine line existed between pleasure and pain. He couldn't remember the last time he'd felt so awful and achy and aroused. "My head is killing me," he complained.

"You can have another dose of ibuprofen in two hours," she informed him. "Until then, just lie still and try not to think too hard."

Good advice, Holden. Don't think. Not about the alluring scent of honeysuckle lingering in her hair. Not about the way her body moves when she leans over the sofa. And definitely not about what could happen now that they were alone together in her apartment.

His fever was obviously making him delirious.

"I feel a little dizzy," he rasped.

"That's not unusual with a temperature of one hundred and two," she replied, wringing out the washcloth in a bowl of cool water and laying it across his forehead again.

"My throat still hurts."

Carly laid one finger over his lips. "Then don't talk so much," she said with a note of exasperation.

The velvet tip of her finger on his mouth startled him into silence. His pulse quickened, escalating the pounding in his ears and his head and his veins, until his entire body reverberated from it.

When she finally freed his lips, he said gruffly, "I'm the one who gives orders around here."

"Not anymore." Her voice sounded gratingly cheerful to his plugged ears. "You've got the flu, Jack. Probably some twenty-four-hour bug that bit you when you weren't looking. So now you're confined to the couch for at least the rest of the day." She fluffed his pillows with cool efficiency. "The tables have turned, Jack Holden. You're in my hands now."

Jack stared at her hands and then shifted beneath his blanket, his fevered brain imagining all sorts of activities for her small, supple hands. Then he ordered himself to stop thinking. Sinking deeper into the sofa, he pulled the blanket up further for protection. "Aren't you afraid that I might be contagious?"

Carly sat down on the edge of the sofa, nudging her hip next to him. "I never get sick. No, really," she added, when he scooted as far away from her as possible. "My brothers caught everything from chicken pox to the croup. I've never even contracted a cold sore."

"Still," he said, his entire body tensing as she shifted on the sofa cushion, "you don't want to take any chances. Especially with the Winsett party on Friday night and the district attorney's fundraiser the day after that."

"I'm not worried." She smiled. "I've got some kind of natural immunity."

"Now I know why you're so fearless," he said dryly. "You think you're immune to everything."

"Only to germs and rules and overprotective men."

"We're not that awful," he retorted hoarsely.

She shuddered. "You can't imagine what it's like growing up in a small town with three big brothers watching my every move. Don't get me wrong," she added quickly. "I really love them. They just drove me crazy. They still do, whenever they get the chance."

"How often is that?"

"Thanksgiving. Christmas. Easter. My folks insist

I come home on major holidays and stay long enough to gain five pounds and hear about all the eligible bachelors in town. I think Mom still harbors the wild hope that I'll find the man of my dreams in North Bend and content myself with catering to him for the rest of my life."

Jack coughed weakly. "Does that mean I need to get my own lunch?"

"I think I can stand waiting on you for one afternoon, especially in your condition."

"Terminal?" he guessed.

"Completely helpless." When she stood up, he noticed the dichotomy of her towering over him. And he didn't like it one bit.

"I'll make you some dry toast and a cup of weak tea," she offered. "How does that sound?"

Jack scowled. "Horrible. How about fried pork rinds and beer?"

Carly firmly shook her head. "No way, Holden. You may find it hard to believe, but I want you to get well." Her eyes narrowed imperceptibly. "The sooner, the better. That means you get tea and toast or else my Mom's favorite flu remedy."

"What's that?" he asked warily.

"Onion gruel. A homemade concoction of onions, milk, and oatmeal. Which, I guarantee you, will make that cough syrup taste like ambrosia." A reminiscent smile curved her lips. "At least, that's what my brothers always told me. Robby, my oldest brother, hated it so much that one time he actually paid me to hide all the onions we had in the house. Of course, my mother didn't let that stop her. We Weiss women always get what we want."

"So, what happened?"

"She used garlic instead," Carly said simply.

Jack shivered beneath his blanket. "Garlic gruel? That definitely sounds like cruel and unusual punishment."

Carly nodded her head in agreement. "Robby never complained about good old onion gruel again. So, Jack," she said, standing up and planting her hands on her hips, "do you still want to argue with me about pork rinds and beer?"

"No, I guess I'll take the dry toast and weak tea," he said with a resigned sigh. "My stomach's growling already."

Twenty minutes later, she set his empty plate on the coffee table and brushed the toast crumbs off the top of the blanket. Then she tucked a crocheted afghan around his feet.

Jack watched her fuss over him. "Why are you being so nice to me?" he asked, hoping his raw throat masked the suspicion edging his words.

Carly avoided his gaze. "Maybe you're just hallucinating," she replied, busying herself with fluffing his pillows once again. "I'd enjoy it while you can."

He wavered between taking her advice or demanding a better explanation. Something inside him warned against pushing her too far and possibly altering this uneasy truce between them. Besides, his wearing nothing but a pair of drawstring athletic shorts underneath the blanket didn't leave him in much of a position to demand anything.

Jack reclined against the pillows, clasping his hands behind his head. More than his suspicions were aroused by her angel of mercy act, but at least he could keep an eye on her this way. "All right, I will. Tell me some more stories about your family."

Carly looked up at him in surprise. Then she shrugged lightly and picked up the washcloth to wring it out once again. "Only if you close your eyes and try to rest."

He dutifully shut his eyes. She obviously hoped to lull him to sleep. Probably with some long, dull story from her youth.

"My Dad is the strong, silent type," she began, gently running the washcloth down the length of his unshaven jaw. "He loves true crime shows and his dream is to someday be called for jury duty. So needless to say, he wasn't too thrilled the summer I got arrested."

Jack's eyes flew open. "Arrested?"

"I'm not saying another word about it until you close your eyes," she admonished, stroking the wash-cloth across his chin.

He closed his eyes again, relaxing beneath the cool cloth and her soft, soothing voice.

"It was a bum rap," she continued.

"That's what they all say," he murmured, his eyes still firmly closed.

"No, I mean that was the charge. I got arrested for vagrancy." She cleared her throat. "And disrupting the peace."

"What happened?" he asked, his voice even again, his eyes closed.

Carly sat in silence for a moment before she resumed her story. "Well, I was working on a school project about panhandling. So, for research purposes, I decided to panhandle on Main Street near Mason's Fruit Stand. Alma helped me with my makeup and costume so no one in town would recognize me."

"And that was enough to fool people?"

"I looked perfect," Carly told him defiantly. "Robby didn't even recognize me when he came to pick me up at the police station."

"I'll bet your family was thrilled."

"Hardly. I was only fifteen years old. Although they understood about the vagrancy mistake."

Jack opened his eyes briefly and then closed them again. "You never did explain about the disturbing the peace charge."

Carly wrung out the washcloth in the water. "It's silly. You don't want to know."

He stifled a yawn. "Sure I do."

"All right. I'll tell you. But only if you promise not to laugh."

"I promise."

"I'm serious, Jack," she warned him. "Even one chuckle and I'll introduce you to onion gruel."

"Now I'm too frightened to even crack a smile. Tell me what happened."

"I got hungry and grabbed an orange from Mason's Fruit Stand." Carly tucked her hair behind her ear. "Panhandling is hard work."

"That sounds more like shoplifting than disturbing the peace."

"I intended to pay for it. Only the next thing I knew there were two hundred oranges rolling down the middle of Main Street. I tried to stop them, but they were faster than I was."

Jack's lips twitched.

"The town smelled like citrus for a week."

A rumble started deep in his chest.

"Don't you dare..." she began.

But it was too late. He burst out laughing. The

vision of two hundred oranges careening down the street with Carly chasing after them proved too much for his endurance. He laughed until his throat grew raw and rough. Until his sides ached as badly as the rest of his body. Until Carly reluctantly joined in with him.

"Well," he said at last, "it seems my laughter, at least, is contagious."

Her indigo eyes balked at his assumption. "Maybe I'm just humoring a dying man."

"Or maybe," Jack challenged, "you're not as immune to me as you think."

Three hours later, while Jack dozed on the sofa, Carly roamed around her small apartment like a blizzard-bound pioneer woman gripped with cabin fever. She'd already dusted from floor to ceiling, alphabetized her recipes, stared at Jack's half-naked body, sent an email to her mother, reorganized her spice rack, and stared at Jack some more.

Now she found herself fighting temptation. Struggling with desire. For pork rinds. Those hunks of crispy, greasy fried pork skin that Jack kept stashed in the cupboard. They'd never appealed to her before.

But the more she tried to forget them, the more persistent her craving grew.

Carly tortured herself even further by walking into the kitchen and opening the fridge to stare at the bulging plastic bag inside. Jack had informed her that the cold temperature kept them from getting rancid. At the time she'd asked him how he could tell the difference. Now she didn't care. She stared at them some more. She wanted one. Desperately.

If only Alma were here to talk her out of it. To tell her all the reasons why eating those pork rinds would be bad for her. A horrible mistake. Especially since Carly had sworn to never let one touch her lips.

She really missed Alma. Missed the cozy chats they used to share when Alma was still speaking to her. How she wished Alma was here now to help her resist temptation. But the only thing between Carly and that cholesterol-laden bag of temptation was a dish of spaetzle. Rusty's spaetzle.

Carly pulled the plastic-wrapped dish from the refrigerator. Jack was supposed to have delivered it this morning, but they both had forgotten about it when he fell ill.

Her dilemma seemed simple enough. Rusty liked his spaetzle fresh. Jack required lots of rest to recover from the flu. And Carly needed a distraction from those beckoning pork rinds. Unfortunately, the solution meant breaking one of Jack's rules.

Carly looked at the spaetzle in her hands, then at the bag of pork rinds, then again at the spaetzle. The quiet apartment enabled her to hear Jack's sonorous breathing in the living room. The cold air from the refrigerator wafted around her, prickling the hair on the back of her neck. Did she dare?

"All this angst for a quick trip across the hall," she muttered under her breath, thoroughly disgusted with herself. She tiptoed across the kitchen, through the living room to the front door. After a furtive glance over her shoulder, she took a deep breath, turned the knob, and walked soundlessly out of the apartment.

The decrepit hallway shone with an aesthetic beauty familiar only to those who know the cruelty of confinement. Carly inhaled the air of freedom, a peculiar blend of insecticide and wet dog hair. Then she walked the short distance to Rusty's door, savoring every unguarded step.

Rusty cracked opened his door just as she raised her hand to knock. "This is a surprise," he announced, sandwiching himself in the narrow opening.

"It's spaetzle day, Rusty," Carly said, holding out

the dish. "I made it just the way you like, with lots of butter and toasted breadcrumbs."

Rusty gazed at her through his thick lenses. "I thought you forgot about me. I never see you anymore."

Carly nibbled her lower lip. "I know. I'm sorry about that." She pushed the dish into his hands. "But I thought about you when I made this."

He stared distastefully down at it. "It seems like the only person you think about anymore is Jack. You spend all your time with him."

"He'll be gone soon, Rusty," Carly assured him. "I promise."

"You promised to let me help you make the next batch of spaetzle too," he replied, shoving the dish back into her hands. "But actions speak louder than words."

Carly stood there in mute disbelief as he shut the door in her face. "Rusty, please," she implored, knocking on the splintered veneer, "let me explain."

But he obviously didn't want any explanations, remaining silent and hidden inside his apartment. Unwilling to hear how her absence from his life wasn't really Jack's fault. She'd hurt him. Just like she'd hurt Alma. Two sensitive people who wouldn't easily forgive her for abandoning them so abruptly.

Carly set the spaetzle down outside his door as a

peace offering, hoping Rusty got to it before the ants did. The thrill of freedom she'd experienced only moments before was now overshadowed by a hollow ache of loneliness.

An ache that didn't subside when she walked back to her apartment, even though she found someone willing to talk to her.

"Where the hell have you been?" Jack growled from the sofa.

She froze in the doorway. "I thought you were asleep."

"Obviously." He struggled to sit up, the blanket falling to his waist. "That was all part of your plan, wasn't it? The bedtime stories. The washcloth. The codeine-laced cough syrup. You wanted to con me into unconsciousness."

"I'm not in the mood for one of your lectures," she clipped, closing the door behind her. "I just came back from Rusty's and he's..."

"Rusty's!" Jack interjected, two red spots burning in his pale cheeks. "You went to Rusty's? Alone?"

"And I lived to tell about it," Carly replied, sinking into the wing chair.

"This time, anyway," Jack retorted. "My instincts tell me there's trouble under that baseball cap. He's the number one suspect on my list."

"You're wrong about Rusty. He's just a sweet,

lonely guy with a few personality problems."

"That's probably what people used to say about Ted Bundy, too. The point is, you're breaking the rules again, Carly. When you break the rules, you face the consequences."

Carly shot to her feet. "You and your rules!" She wrenched her gaze away from the muscles rippling across his broad, naked chest and unleashed her frustration. "They might have cost me my best friend and my best neighbor, who's so dangerous he scrapes ice off my car windows in the winter and grows endive on his balcony for me in the summer. As far as I'm concerned, Jack Holden, you can take your rules and stick them where I should have stuck that thermometer!"

Before he could say another word, Carly flounced out of the living room and into the kitchen. Grabbing a beer out of the refrigerator, she popped the tab, her gaze falling on the bag of pork rinds as she took a long draught. Wiping her foamy lip with the back of her hand, she picked up the unopened bag and dumped them in the trash can, not even bothering to consider the consequences of her actions.

After all, Jack had already insulted one catering customer, punched another, tricked her into a pair of handcuffs, and alienated her friends. What more could he do to her now?

7

Less than a week to go.

Jack comforted himself with this thought as he drove the car around to the back entrance of the remote Winsett estate. A long, winding road bordered on both sides by towering cedar trees surrounded the rambling, nineteenth century brick house. The moonless night and a thick fog contributed to the eerie atmosphere of the August evening.

Once outside, a chill prickled up Jack's spine as he stumbled over the thick, dormant branches of overgrown rose bushes snaking out over the cobblestones, as if they were hands reaching out to hinder his entry into the house.

His undue apprehension didn't subside once inside the large well-lit kitchen. Setting down the load of covered trays in his arms, he swore softly under his breath for letting Carly have her way. Again.

It was becoming a bad habit with him, looking into those big blue eyes while she persuaded him to let her run around Pine City with a possible homicidal stalker on her heels. Or drop her off at the front door so she could receive last-minute instructions from the Winsetts while Jack used the servants' entrance.

A harmless indulgence, considering he'd checked out the house and the grounds before he let Carly out of the car. Niles Winsett checked out, too, according to Jack's sources. A mild-mannered businessman with no history of psychological problems or known associations with Professor Chester Frey. So there really wasn't any reason to worry.

Jack blamed his uneasiness on exhaustion. Last night he'd lain awake into the wee hours of the night, contemplating the pros and cons of using coriander when making pesto. A month ago, he didn't even know what coriander was. Or pesto, for that matter. Now he couldn't stop thinking about it. Of course, if he was honest with himself, it was Carly that he couldn't keep out of his mind.

He'd been tough on her lately. Okay, more than tough. Those handcuffs might have been overdoing it a bit. And Alma still refused to talk to her. Even Rusty made him look like the bad guy, no longer leaving his newspaper outside Carly's door.

Jack hadn't intended to make her life completely miserable. It just seemed to turn out that way. When he wasn't irritating her, she was frustrating him. Or tempting him. He found it a daily struggle to maintain the cool, aloof demeanor that had earned him his hard-won reputation as one of the top bodyguards in North Texas. But the real struggle was keeping his distance from Carly now that they were alone together in her apartment.

Jack heaved a frazzled sigh as he unstacked the trays.

On Monday the trial would begin, and Carly would be called to testify. And he'd finally be free to tend to his cattle instead of a tempestuous caterer. Maybe he just needed distance from her to break this perplexing hold she seemed to have on him.

Taking off his cowboy hat, he hung it on a hook next to the door. Then he glanced at his watch. Fifteen minutes had passed since she'd told him to unload the car, then disappeared inside this mausoleum. He scowled. Maybe this Niles Winsett wasn't as harmless as she believed. Maybe the man's polite behavior at the coffee shop had all been part of a calculated plan. Maybe...

Before he could imagine the worst, the object of his frustration breezed in from the dining hall and brushed past him to the kitchen sink.

"What is that?" he asked, his mouth dry.

"What?" Carly replied, rubbing the soap on her hands into a lather.

"That thing you're wearing."

After drying her hands on a dish towel, she smoothed down the obscenely short skirt with obvious pleasure. "It's my costume." She twirled daintily on one foot. "How do I look?"

"Like Lady Godiva without the horse." His disbelieving gaze fell from the snug red peasant blouse, worn off the shoulders to reveal the generous swell of her breasts, past the skimpy skirt to the black fishnet stockings encasing her long, shapely legs. He hadn't noticed any costume when they'd left the apartment. Which meant she must have brought it with her and changed while he was parking her car.

"Costume? What exactly is going on here, Carly?"

"Did I forget to mention that this is sort of a masquerade party?"

"You certainly did. And what do you mean by 'sort of'?"

She wrinkled her pert nose. "It's complicated."

"Try me."

"The Winsetts are hosting a murder mystery

party for their fifteenth anniversary. Each of the guests is given a role to perform throughout the evening. After Mrs. Winsett, who plays the victim, falls down dead in the vichyssoise, the game begins. Then certain clues are revealed during the dinner until the murderer is revealed."

"You're kidding."

She actually grinned at him. "I'm Colette. The French actress masquerading as a maid so that I can finally confront the woman who abandoned me at birth all those years ago. She is now a famous doctor. The head of a world-renowned infertility clinic in Switzerland."

"You have a role, too?" he asked wryly.

"*Oui*," she replied, in the most atrocious French accent he'd ever heard.

He still couldn't wrench his gaze from her revealing outfit. "And that's all you're going to wear?"

Her blue eyes widened. "Oh, I almost forgot." Reaching into the pocket of a minuscule lace apron tied around her slim waist, Carly retrieved a perky red bow and pinned it atop her tousled chestnut curls. Then she found a mirror and darkened the beauty spot on her left cheek with an eyebrow pencil. "There. That's much better."

He didn't know whether to laugh or throw a coat over her.

Carly sidled next to him, a mischievous smile playing about the corners of her mouth. "*Bonjour.*" She pronounced it banjo. Draping the length of her partially clad body against his, she murmured, "My name is Colette, and you are...?" Her finger teased along the length of his jaw.

"Furious that you didn't tell me about all this before we got here."

"Wrong." She pulled a small index card from the pocket of her apron and began reading from it. "You're Humphrey, the long-suffering butler. He's dour and morose. He's also a kleptomaniac, frequently stealing from his employer and the guests."

"You expect me to go along with this nonsense, too?"

"It's all part of the job." She slid the card into the pocket of his black dinner jacket and gave it a gentle pat. "You should see Mrs. Winsett. She is wearing the most gorgeous blue sequined gown with matching spiked heels. They must be at least four inches high. If she falls off them, she'll break her neck."

"That hardly seems to matter," Jack quipped, "since she'll be dead after the first course."

Carly unwrapped the pan of vichyssoise. "Good point. Try not to trip over her body when you serve the rest of the meal. And don't forget the clues."

"Clues?" he echoed, distracted by the fluid movement of her hips beneath the shifting fabric of her miniskirt.

"One after each course. You'll give them to Niles, alias Colonel Lippy, on the silver salver." She grimaced. "Silver salver. Try saying that three times fast."

Jack looked up. "What?"

"Never mind," she replied, carefully ladling the chilled soup into gold-rimmed china bowls. "Just remember to present a clue to the colonel after the guests have finished each course."

"Who's the colonel?"

Carly heaved a patient sigh as she set a fresh sprig of parsley atop each bowl. "Mr. Winsett is playing the role of Colonel Lippy. Mrs. Winsett plays the colonel's wife."

"The murder victim," Jack said quickly, to show her he was paying attention.

"Right." She placed the bowls on a large round tray. "The one poisoned by the vichyssoise. The rest of the guests will fill the roles of a professional golfer, a movie actress, an author, the world-famous doctor I told you about..."

"Colette's birth mother," he interjected.

Carly nodded and leaned forward to drop a small

curtsey, giving him a provocative view of her gaping neckline.

That did it. Jack reached over and tugged up both sleeves of her peasant blouse, raising the bodice up a good two inches on her chest.

"Jack!" she cried, grasping at the blouse with one hand.

"The name's Humphrey," he growled. "And if you curtsey like that in the dining hall, there won't be any mystery left. At least not about you, Mademoiselle Colette."

Carly laughed as a delicate pink blush stained her cheeks. "That's wonderful! You make a perfect Humphrey. The scowl. The tone of your voice. Even the way you clench your teeth together when you talk."

Jack grasped her roughly by her bare shoulders. "Perhaps there's more to Humphrey than meets the eye." He drew her closer to him as a gasp of surprise escaped her lips. "Perhaps I am not really a butler, but the long-lost..." His eyes swept her face as he inhaled the delicate scent of her familiar perfume. Resisting the urge to explore more of the petal soft skin beneath his hands, Jack headed out of dangerous territory. "...brother of Colette. Searching the ends of the earth for my beloved sister so that I may give her what she desires most." He paused a beat. "Sanctuary in a convent."

"Brother?" Carly echoed, obviously disappointed.

Jack shrugged. "Uncle, maybe?"

Licking her lips, she leaned into him, purposely pressing herself against his chest. "How about lover," she murmured huskily. "The man who invades my dreams every night, who fills my every waking thought. I have missed you, *mi amore*."

"That's Italian, not French."

Carly shrugged as she wound her arms around his neck. "Colette spent her formative years in northern Italy, studying the great masters of painting and sculpture."

"I've heard you get around, mademoiselle."

An enigmatic smile curved her lips. "Looking for the man who stole my heart."

Jack cleared his throat as her fingers danced through his hair. He reminded himself that she was just pretending. An actress perfecting her craft. This was Colette talking, the hot coquette. Not Carly, the caterer, the con artist, the witness under his protection. This was Colette teasing and touching him so provocatively that his arms ached with the urge to crush her against him.

"Well, after all," he said. "Humphrey is a kleptomaniac. He can't help himself."

"I hope not," she murmured seductively.

Jack swallowed. His gaze fell to her parted lips. He tried to ignore how full they were... and soft... and moist. He tried to forget how hot and succulent her kisses had been against his mouth.

He closed his eyes as her hand slowly roamed the hard lines of his chest until it crept beneath his dinner jacket and rested above his pounding heart. He stopped breathing as his body tightened at her touch.

"Do you steal only hearts, Humphrey? Or kisses, too?"

Jack drew in a sharp breath. "Kisses, mademoiselle? I'm not sure I understand."

She gazed at him through the thick fringe of her lowered lashes. "Then perhaps I should show you what I mean." Crooking one finger, she whispered, "Come a little closer, *por favor*."

His gray eyes locked on her blue ones. "That's Spanish, my sweet Colette. Fortunately, for you," he said, leaning toward her, "I'm multilingual."

"This will require no translation," she said huskily. "It is a language known around the world." Standing on tiptoe, she lifted her face toward his, her soft breath fluttering against his mouth like the wings of a hummingbird.

"Carly," he groaned, her name both a plea and

a curse. Capturing her mouth with his own, he plundered its warm depths. She stilled for a moment at the onslaught, then her lips softened and parted, welcoming the invasion. Jack lost himself as he pulled her to him, his blood thrumming in his ears, his body hard and hot. Nothing mattered to him except quenching his thirst for her. Not the dinner party or the overheated kitchen or his cold, unyielding rules. Not the future or the past, only this timeless moment between them.

Her head fell back, allowing his lips to continue their exploration along the long, slender column of her neck until he reached her proud chin and found her supple mouth once more. She leaned into him, creating the most sensual, erotic, frustrating sensation Jack had ever experienced.

And they were still standing in the middle of the darn kitchen.

Framing her face between his hands, he lifted his head and saw the banked fires in her eyes. They drew him, like a moth to the flames, until his forehead rested on hers.

"Now what?" he asked, his breathing ragged.

Carly tried to steady herself without reaching for him. That way lay madness. This whole scheme she concocted to get him to kiss her again was mad.

Crazy. Totally insane. Even if she did still tingle down to her toes.

"Wait a minute," she said, trying to catch her breath and not hyperventilate at the same time. "I have to think."

A smile tipped up one corner of his mouth as he lifted his head away from hers. "That always seems to lead to trouble."

Tell me about it. Her carefully constructed plan to act the coquette and conquer his defenses worked beautifully. Except for the grand finale. The moment when she would look deep into his eyes and say, "Gotcha!" But that moment came and went. She didn't want revenge anymore. Or another apology.

She only wanted Jack.

That thought terrified her more than anything ever had. "I think we need to talk," she began.

Niles Winsett chose that moment to march into his kitchen. "The guests are all here!" His army boots clattered on the tile floor as he strode over to the counter and perused the array of dishes scattered across it. "Heavenly," he said, inhaling the savory aroma of roasting beef. "When do we eat?"

Carly wanted to scream at the intrusion. Or garrote the man with her garter belt. Instead, she pushed herself away from Jack, her fingers flexing against the hard muscles of his chest.

"Jack will serve the first course whenever you're ready," Carly said, trying to sound like the consummate professional while she twisted her peasant blouse back into position.

"Not Jack," Niles reminded her with a sly smile. "Humphrey. His name is Humphrey." He stood at attention, the medals on his khaki uniform tinkling with importance. "You are Colette and I'm Colonel Lippy. For this evening to be a success, everyone must perform their part to perfection."

"We've just been rehearsing," Jack said, straightening his bow tie. "Carly's got the part of Colette down pat."

"Wonderful," Niles replied. "Well, you know what they say, practice makes perfect. And perfection is what Marguerite and I expect. We take great pride in our murder mystery parties."

Carly turned to unwrap the Yorkshire pudding. She needed to keep her mind, as well as her hands, off Jack. For the sake of her business if not her sanity.

"I know the food will be perfect," she assured Niles, her voice unnaturally husky. She cleared her throat. "A traditional English meal, with all the trimmings."

"Excellent, Colette," Niles murmured, rubbing his hands together. "But what about the clues? Does Humphrey have them?"

Jack reached for the small bundle of white sealed envelopes on the counter. "Right here."

"They're numbered chronologically," Niles warned. "It would be a disaster if they were opened out of order."

"Luckily for you, Colonel, counting is one of my many skills."

Carly's gaze fell to Jack's hands as she wondered just what other skills he possessed. A warm heat spread through her body as she imagined the possibilities.

"All right, then." Niles clomped over to the door. "Let's begin. Please remember to remain in character throughout the evening."

"*Oui, monsieur*," Carly said in unintelligible French.

"What?" Niles asked, looking to Jack for a translation.

Jack assumed an air of dignified disdain appropriate for a long-suffering butler. Unfortunately, his rumpled hair and the smudge of red lipstick on his jaw ruined the effect. "Colette simply means everything is under control."

Carly took a deep breath, wishing it was true.

"Very well, then," Niles muttered, looking around the large kitchen as if he'd misplaced something. "Humphrey, I believe we're ready for the first course."

Jack picked up the tray off the counter, tilting it

slightly as he lifted it to shoulder level. Soup splashed over the edge of each bowl.

Niles clicked his tongue. "None of that now, Humphrey. I don't want anything to upset my darling Marguerite tonight. After all, she is allowing me to murder her for our fifteenth anniversary. Even if it is a rather tame poisoning instead of a good stabbing or strangulation." He sighed regretfully and then turned on his booted heel and left the room.

Jack lowered the tray far enough for Carly to dab up the spilt soup with a paper towel. "You're shaking," he said, catching her fingers in his hand.

"Colette is jittery," she explained weakly, pulling away from him.

"Chilly, too, no doubt," he observed, his gaze lingering on her scantily clad body. Then his eyes once again met hers and held. They stared at one another for a long, silent moment. "Maybe you'd better stay here in the kitchen where it's warm."

"Is that an order?" she challenged, reaching up to wipe the lipstick off his face with the edge of the paper towel.

Jack smiled at the familiar defiance in her eyes. But he didn't rise to the bait. "Yes," he replied softly. "Remember that my role, first and foremost, is to protect you from harm."

"I'm in no danger," she lied, looking into the

steely eyes of the most dangerous threat to her equilibrium in her entire life.

One corner of his mouth tilted into a nostalgic smile. "I didn't foresee much danger from Bobby Joe Hodges. But as you know from firsthand experience, sometimes danger appears when you least expect."

Carly closed her eyes. "I don't like rats."

Jack frowned down at the tray in his arms, wishing they were free to hold her once again. "I know," he said softly. "Just remember that they come in all shapes and sizes."

With that, he waltzed into the dining hall and ran smack into Professor Chester Frey.

Carly stood in the middle of the empty kitchen, rubbing her hands vigorously up and down her bare arms. She couldn't seem to stop shaking. And that wasn't her only symptom. She felt disoriented. Breathless. Wired. Like she'd just overdosed on double-fudge brownies.

What was the matter with her?

The sound of shattering china, followed by the clang of the metal tray and the heavy thud of bodies hitting the floor gave her the answer she didn't want. She moaned and closed her eyes. *Not again.*

Jack.

He was the source of all her problems. He was the most sexy, overprotective, uncoordinated man she'd ever met. And she was falling for him. The awful truth hit her like the blast of heat from a five-hundred-degree oven.

Carly gripped the edge of the counter and tried to talk herself out of it. *Not Jack. Anyone but Jack.* Not only was it an impossible dream, but it was also her worst nightmare. She wanted to fall in love. Someday. When her catering business was secure and her life on track. With someone who was sensitive and accommodating and housebroken.

Not with Jack Holden. The man who had handcuffed her when she wandered away from him for half an hour. The man who had a list of rules for every occasion. She couldn't fall for someone who ate pork rinds on purpose. And shaved only on the days with the letter *T* in them. And scorched her ninety-five-dollar saute pan. Even if he did make her melt at his feet when he touched her.

She shivered at the vision of herself at his feet. *Just where he wanted her.* Of course, if his feet were as sexy as the rest of him...

A woman's muffled scream opened her eyes. Literally.

Here she was fantasizing about Jack's feet while

he was out there tripping over her customers. Presenting as much of a danger to her business as her heart.

Carly ran for the door of the dining hall, determined not to lose either one.

"You clumsy oaf!" shouted a portly gentleman sporting a gray three-piece suit, silver-rimmed reading glasses, and a well-trimmed goatee. He sat on the floor among splintered shards of bone china and lumpy pools of vichyssoise.

Jack's heart hammered against his chest. Frey! The man was supposed to be locked in a jail cell, not dining in a secluded house on the outskirts of Pine City. Not anywhere near Carly.

His reflexes soon overcame his shock as he reached inside his dinner jacket for his concealed gun. That's when he saw one end of the white mustache dangling from the upper lip of the enraged guest. And when he noticed that the beady eyes behind the reading glasses weren't a soulless brown but a mossy green.

"Imbecile!" snarled the man, his fake mustache falling to the floor as he clambered to his feet. He kicked the hairy nosepiece viciously against the wall, splattering soup everywhere. "You've ruined my finest waistcoat. Not to mention the first course."

"Who are you?" Jack demanded, leaving his gun in place. For now.

"Insolent, too! For your information, I am Professor Chester Frey."

A woman's shrill, stifled scream punctuated the name.

Tiny hairs prickled on the back of Jack's neck. The man not only dressed as Frey but also claimed his identity. This murder mystery party was becoming more messed up by the moment.

"Tell me, Colonel Lippy," said the faux professor as Niles Winsett appeared at his side, "why do you tolerate this servant's impertinence? I always deal swiftly with those who fail to show me the proper respect."

"The soup!" Niles gasped as he watched the milky liquid run in between the cracks of the hardwood floor. "It's ruined. Gone." He raised horrified eyes to Jack, clutching at his sleeve. "My wife is *dying* for a bowl of vichyssoise, Humphrey. What do you propose we do now?"

Jack knew exactly what he wanted to do. Gather up Carly and her catering gear and get as far away from this crazy party as possible. These people not only found murder entertaining, they dressed up as homicidal killers.

"Humphrey?" prompted Niles, now wringing his hands together. "Do you have any suggestions?" The remaining guests sat around the dinner table in stony silence. "Any suggestions at all?" he finished weakly.

The kitchen door swung open. "What happened...?" Carly's words trailed off as she caught site of the soup pooling on the floor.

Then her gaze rose to observe the wet stains darkening the waistcoat of the man imitating Professor Frey. The professional smile faded from her blanched lips, now almost as white as her face. "What's going on here?" she whispered.

"Isn't it obvious?" grumbled the faux professor. "This incompetent butler decided to serve me the first course. Unfortunately, I'm wearing it instead of eating it."

Carly began breathing again when she realized the man in front of her wasn't Chester Frey. "The vichyssoise," she said, trying to recover her composure.

"Yes, the vichyssoise," echoed Niles, nervously wringing his hands together. "The dish my dear wife is *dying* for. I only hope you have some left in that kitchen of yours, Colette, or you'll wish you were dead!"

Carly swallowed. Without the vichyssoise there

could be no murder. Without a murder, no murder mystery party. And without a party, no future business opportunities for Carly's Creations.

Jack gripped her elbow. "Come along, Colette. Let's go dish up some more soup."

She frowned up at him. He knew perfectly well there was no more vichyssoise. And judging by the implacable expression on his face, he didn't care. If she left the room with him now, she knew she'd never see Niles Winsett or his promised catering contract again.

"Humphrey, please," she implored, wriggling out of his grasp. Then she smiled at the guests seated around the table, most of them glaring at her. She took a deep breath and tried desperately to think of some way to save the situation.

"It is a very special recipe," Carly began, in her best imitation of a French accent. "It calls for rare herbs found onlee in a tiny shop in thee heart of Neepples."

"Nipples?" Mrs. Winsett gasped.

"I believe she means Naples," Jack said impatiently. "Mademoiselle Colette studied in Italy as a child."

"*Oui*," Carly affirmed, then decided to forgo the French accent before things got any worse. "I only had enough herbs for eight servings of vichyssoise."

Niles Winsett groaned. One of the guests, dressed in a doctor's white lab coat with a paper stethoscope pinned to the collar, tossed her linen napkin on the table in disgust.

"Such a shame," Carly improvised. "I'm certain it was delicious. Didn't you think so, Mrs. Lippy?"

All eyes in the room turned to Mrs. Niles Winsett. Her hand fluttered to her throat. "Me?"

"Yes," Carly said, nodding her head. "You came into the kitchen earlier this evening for a taste. Remember?"

Mrs. Winsett's face remained blank.

"You told me to add a pinch more pepper," Carly prodded, wondering if the woman would catch on in time to save her from another catering disaster.

"Yes... I think I remember now," Mrs. Winsett said vaguely.

"You've been looking a little pale ever since," Carly said to the intended victim. "Are you not feeling well?"

"Oh!" Niles Winsett clapped his hands in delight as he turned to his wife. "So, you sampled the vichyssoise, after all. Yes, my dearest, you do look absolutely awful."

"I have been feeling rather ill," Mrs. Winsett said with more conviction. "Very ill, in fact. Ever since I sampled that soup." She stood up, gripping the back of her chair with one hand. Wobbling on her high heels, she lifted one hand to her brow. "It must have been... poisoned." With a fake moan of agony, she crumpled to the floor, moving only long enough to pull the hem of her dress over her knees and pillow her head underneath one arm. Then she lay still as a sequined corpse.

Carly inwardly breathed a sigh of relief. She'd cleared the first hurdle.

"Humphrey," Niles called from the head of the table. "My dear wife has suffered the most horrendous death. Naturally, no one can leave this house until the killer is caught."

"That's your cue," Carly whispered to Jack. "Give him the first clue."

A muscle twitched in Jack's jaw as he stared at her.

Carly suppressed a shiver when she saw the raw emotions swirling in those murky gray depths. Emotions she couldn't let sway her. "Please, Jack," she pleaded under her breath.

He turned abruptly away from her and grabbed the silver salver off the sideboard. "The first clue," he muttered, placing the envelope marked Number One on the small tray before presenting it to Niles. "Let's hurry up and read it so we can discover who killed my mistress."

Carly breathed a deep sigh of relief.

"Your mistress!" The faux professor rubbed his hands together. "I see we have a suspect in this case already, Colonel. Did you know you'd been cuckolded by your own butler?"

She almost groaned aloud when she realized she forgot to tell Jack that the players could improvise at any time, as long as they remained true to character. The guests seated around the dining table looked at one another with an air of eager anticipation. Jack looked at Carly as if he wanted to handcuff her again.

"I can't believe it, Humphrey," Niles sputtered. "How long have you been conducting this affair with my wife?"

"Don't be ridiculous," Jack replied. "I'm not having an affair with your wife."

"Not anymore," chimed a guest, wielding a putting iron in one hand. "She's dead now. And either you killed her, or perhaps"—his gaze roamed over the other guests in the room—"her death was caused by someone in a jealous rage."

Carly held her breath as the murder mystery party gained momentum. So far, so good. Mrs. Winsett, aka Mrs. Lippy, was playing dead, the spilt vichyssoise forgotten. And Jack hadn't punched anyone yet.

Niles rose to his feet, an enthusiastic sparkle in his eyes. "Do you dare accuse me, sir?" He stepped over the inert body of his wife to confront the golfer. "Mrs. Lippy was the love of my life."

"Exactly," the golfer replied, his brow furrowed with speculation. "That's why you couldn't stand the thought of her giving herself to another man."

"Jealousy is a powerful motive," Carly piped in, eager to add to the entertainment. "Not only for a man, but a woman as well. Humphrey admitted to me earlier that he's not above stealing hearts."

Jack looked at Carly as if she were out of her mind. Fortunately, she was used to that particular expression on his face.

The faux Professor Frey smiled at Carly as he wiped at the wet spots on his suit with a handkerchief. "You are so perceptive, mademoiselle. Jealousy can make a woman... or a man do... just about anything. Even murder."

Jack's eyes fixed on the impostor. "Care to elaborate?" he asked, his voice dangerously quiet.

Carly stepped forward and placed a restraining hand on Jack's arm. "No one can expect to solve a murder on an empty stomach," she said brightly. "Shall we serve the next course, Humphrey?"

"First I'd like to hear *Professor Frey's* views on the matter."

She didn't like that suspicious gleam in his eye. Or the bulge of his gun under his jacket. "We're the hired help," she whispered under her breath, "not the stars of the show. So, please don't say another word or you'll get us both fired."

"You'd be wise to listen to your little French pastry," chimed the faux professor. He took a step toward her, licking his thin lips as his eyes flickered over the length of her. "Such a delectable creature. Made of sugar, spice, and everything nice."

"That's it," Jack clipped. He marched up to the impostor and seized him by the lapel of his soiled waistcoat. "You're going to jail."

"Humphrey!" Carly exclaimed with horror.

Niles pounded on the table. "You can't accuse him of my wife's murder yet! We haven't even read the first clue."

The other guests joined in the protest, shouting, clanging silverware, and surrounding Carly to beseech her to control her catering assistant. She rose on her tiptoes to see over the people crowding around her, trying to catch Jack's eye. "Humphrey, I think you're making a big mistake," she yelled above the din.

And then it was suddenly very quiet. Jack had silenced them all by handcuffing the Chester Frey imposter. "The party's over, folks," Jack announced, then turned to Carly. "Call the police."

Carly swallowed a groan of despair. Jack had ruined everything. Again.

8

"You're off the case," D.A. Monica Boyle announced as soon as Jack walked through the door of her office.

He stopped short at her words. Then he realized what they meant. "That Frey phony confessed to writing those notes, didn't he?"

"Close the door."

Pushing it shut behind him, he approached her desk with one hand curled into a fist. "I knew it. The moment I laid eyes on that creep I knew he was the one threatening Carly."

The satisfaction that flowed through him ebbed when he noticed the sour expression puckering the D.A.'s face. If he didn't know better, he'd almost think she was serious about that "off the case" crack.

"That *creep* you arrested is the president of Eastside Bank," she informed him dryly. "Hubert Hagerty is a harmless, upstanding citizen who spends his spare time raising purebred Pomeranians. He also happens to be a major contributor to my reelection campaign. Or should I say, used to be a major contributor."

Jack sat down in a chair directly across from her desk and leaned back. "The last time I checked, cash donations don't make a person immune from prosecution."

"And last time I checked," she countered, "the police had found nothing but dog hair and a clean record on Hagerty. Nothing to link him to the threats against Carly."

Her tone disturbed him even more than her words. "Don't tell me they let him go?"

"Ten minutes ago." She tossed her pen onto the desk. "We didn't have any reason to hold him, Jack, other than your instincts. And as hard as it is to believe, most judges frown on that sort of evidence." An exasperated sigh escaped her. "You blew it tonight. Big-time. What were you thinking?"

He'd been thinking about heating up that kitchen with Carly. But that wasn't the answer Monica wanted to hear, and he didn't want to admit it. Especially to himself. That brief interlude as Humphrey and

Colette was a one-time performance. A lapse in judgment he blamed on the theatrical blood in his veins. Courtesy of his Grandma Hattie, who in her younger years had starred in the Pine City Women's Club production of *Oklahoma*.

"I assessed the situation and decided not to take any chances with the witness under my protection." *Very convincing, Holden. Keep it up.* "Call me crazy, but I found Hagerty's impersonation of Frey more than a little suspicious."

"It was a costume party," Monica reminded him crisply. "Carly Weiss was dressed in a skimpy French maid costume, but I didn't see you arresting her for indecent exposure."

Jack remembered just how exposed to him she'd been, her skin hot and soft as silk beneath his hands. How arresting her had been the last thing on his mind. "The man identified himself as Frey. What was I supposed to do, wait until he shot up the dessert cart to prove the resemblance?"

Monica snorted. "Mrs. Niles Winsett lay like a corpse on the floor, but nobody phoned for an ambulance. It's called acting, Jack. Fun and games. You should try it sometime."

He didn't bother to tell her about Humphrey's debut, a character without any self-control. "I didn't like the role Hagerty played. Or the way he said his line."

Monica arched a silver brow. "Which one? '*I'm planning to sue the city for false arrest*?' Or: '*So help me, Monica, I'll make certain you're never reelected to this office again*.'"

Jack leaned forward. "How about referring to Carly as '*made of sugar and spice and everything nice*'? That's a direct quote from the first anonymous threat." He glanced at the assortment of papers littering her desk. "Didn't you read about it in my report?"

"Yes. But it's hardly a smoking gun."

"Maybe not, although it seems like an odd coincidence. I hope you didn't let Hagerty go on the strength of his bank account, Monica. Losing a campaign contribution is nothing compared to losing Carly."

"We won't lose her. The trial starts on Monday and the odds for a successful prosecution are highly in our favor. She'll be safe without you until then."

Jack couldn't believe his ears. "This is actually the most dangerous time—she'll be testifying soon. Is placating your political cronies really worth the risk?"

Her mouth hardened. "You're not the only one capable of protecting Carly. I sent her home a little while ago with Ted Simmons."

"Too Tired Ted?" he scoffed, suddenly feeling like a kid stuck at the top of a Ferris wheel. She actually meant it. He was off the case. "He retired from Tuf Security because he couldn't keep his eyes open between naps."

"He's not that bad. Besides, it's the weekend. He's the best I could find on such short notice. At least he's qualified for the job."

"Why even bother looking for someone else when I'm right here? Ready, willing, and a hell of a lot more able than Simmons."

Resentment flared within him that he and Carly were obviously nothing but pawns in her political games. Taking him off the case amounted to a public office ploy designed to satisfy Hagerty's ruffled pride. A ploy that filled him with apprehension when he thought of Carly without adequate protection. Without him.

"Look, my interaction with Hagerty is hardly a secret," he told her. "People at the party posted videos of him in handcuffs to their social media accounts before we even left the house."

Monica rubbed her temple with her fingertips. "Don't remind me. I've done nothing but damage control all evening."

"So why make matters worse by removing me from the case?"

"It's not my decision," she said wearily.

Jack rubbed one hand over his jaw. "Then whose is it? Hagerty's? Your campaign manager's? Or is Chester Frey calling the shots now from his jail cell?"

"It's Carly's."

Her name hit him like a sucker punch to the gut. He blinked and fell back a step.

"For some reason, she doesn't want your protection anymore."

"She hasn't wanted my protection from day one," he said, numb with shock. "It's the main topic of conversation every night at the dinner table."

"This time she means it," the district attorney replied. "Demands it, actually. I won't go into all the details, but she wants you off the case, Jack. Effective immediately."

"You can't be serious."

"Dead serious. If you'll pardon the expression."

"Interesting choice of words," he mused. "Did you happen to mention that possibility to Carly when she made her request?"

"It didn't seem to concern her as much as never wanting to see you again."

Jack sat down in the nearest chair, trying to make sense of it all. "Sounds like I shouldn't ask her for a letter of reference." He knew she'd been upset about the curtailed catering gig, but not this upset. Not upset enough to convince the D.A. to bring in a second-string bodyguard. "I thought you and Carly had a deal—catering your fundraiser luncheon in exchange for me."

"I can't back out of my side of it at this late date," she told him. "I'd never find someone else to handle a sit-down dinner for one hundred people with less than twenty-four hours' notice. At least I convinced her to accept Ted in your place."

"Ted Simmons isn't the man for the job."

"Well, for some reason neither are you. I don't know what happened between you two, but she seems different somehow. If I didn't know better, I'd say she was frightened of you." Her gaze flicked over him. "And I don't think it's your gun that scares her."

"Nothing scares Carly," he exclaimed. "That's why I don't understand..." Then it hit him. Like the kick from a double-barreled shotgun.

You're going to pay for this, Jack.

So, it hadn't been an empty threat. And she'd gotten him just where she wanted. Off the case. Spoiling his perfect record and wreaking her revenge all in one shot.

Frustration mounted within him as he thought of everything, he'd endured the last few weeks because of her. The topless bachelorette party fiasco. The concealed evidence. The flu. Which might not technically be her fault, but he'd bet money she'd enjoyed watching him suffer.

Then the grand finale. Her flirtatious performance as Colette. His body tightened at the memory. Was that one of the *details* Monica didn't want to share? Did Carly include his amorous misconduct among her litany of complaints?

Eight years in the bodyguard business and he'd finally met his match. A woman who delivered a knockout punch that left him reeling. Only he wasn't down for the count. Not yet.

Jack stood up. "I've got to go."

Monica rose to her feet to stop him, but he was already halfway out the door. "Stay away from her, Jack," she called after him, her tone conveying a direct order.

An order he didn't intend to obey.

Peace and quiet weren't the standard fare at the Sagebrush Apartments after midnight. Country music emanated from a nearby tavern, often accompanied by the occasional howling alley cat or pickup truck drag race.

Carly usually slept through it all. But tonight, she lay awake, tossing and turning in her double bed. She could hear Ted's strangled snores in her living room and wondered if trading Jack in for an older model still made sense.

Business-wise, of course, it was a sound decision. Carly's Creations couldn't handle any more help from Jack Holden, unless he started working for the competition.

He'd cost her customers, credibility, and peace of mind.

That's why choosing Ted to protect her from herself had seemed like the right decision. He was older, duller, and infinitely safer. Unless she died of boredom.

A sharp rap on the front door delayed that possibility. Maybe it was all her former catering customers, coming to tell her they couldn't eat another bite without her. Or Rusty, returning the spaetzle dish and resuming their friendship. Or Jack. Anxious to jump all over her. Figuratively, of course. She had no doubt he was furious with her for going over his head.

Carly clutched the edge of the cotton blanket and drew it up around her as the rapping grew more persistent. Maybe if she just lay here long enough the unwelcome visitor would get the hint. That hope faded when the rapping progressed to a break-down-the-door pounding. She scrambled out of bed before all the commotion woke Ted Van Winkle and hurried to open it.

Jack stood on the other side.

"If you're here to apologize," she said, her heart racing, "I'll take a rain check."

Jack looked as though he had no intention of apologizing. His midnight-black hair was slicked back, his unshaven jaw set in a firm line, and his steel-gray eyes smoldered with lethal intensity. "I'll take an explanation," he demanded.

"I don't give explanations to men over six feet tall." Carly gazed up at him. "I've got a rule against it."

The contours of his face hardened. "Believe it or not, I'm in a rule-breaking mood. Now are you going to invite me in, or do you prefer the privacy of the hallway?"

Carly stepped into the hall, closing the door firmly behind her. It had been hard enough getting Jack out of her apartment in the first place. She didn't know if she had the strength or the willpower to do it a second time.

"It's quieter out here," she told him. "Ted snores and he's sleeping on a board propped between two chairs in my living room. We'd never be able to hear each other over all the racket."

Jack's eyes burned into her. "Why, Carly?"

She shrugged. "My guess is a deviated septum. Although I've heard snoring can also be caused by nasal polyps or even allergies."

"That's not what I meant, and you know it."

Of course she knew it. She just didn't want to make it easy for him. Not when living without him seemed like the hardest prospect she'd ever faced. Almost as hard as living with him. Following his rules. Fighting for her independence and the television remote control.

"Do I?" she asked innocently.

"Don't play dumb with me," he warned with menacing softness. "You're smart, Carly. Maybe too darn smart for your own good."

"That's the nicest thing you've ever said to me, Jack. So unexpected, too. The way you've ordered me around in the past few weeks, I naturally assumed you thought my brain was malfunctioning."

He took a step toward her. "I'll admit I underestimated you."

"Happens all the time."

"Not to me." Jack advanced another step, and then a third.

Carly slowly backed up until she hit drywall, silently blasting herself for retreating. "Consider yourself lucky. Now that you're off the case, you don't have to deal with me anymore."

"Except that we've got some unfinished business."

Adrenaline shot through her in a fight-or-flight response. He stood so close that the only place she could fly was into his arms. A few more trips there and she'd qualify for frequent flyer miles, but with a broken heart as the final destination. So she chose to fight instead.

"Too late," she said. "It's long after midnight and you should be long gone by now. I don't have to listen to you anymore."

He gave a short, sharp laugh. "As if you ever listened to me! And in case you haven't noticed, I'm still here."

She noticed. It explained the crick in her neck. And the fact that every fiber in her being vibrated with a feverish intensity at his nearness. "If you've come for your stuff, I already routed it back to the D.A.'s office."

"I've come for an explanation," he growled. "You owe me that."

She squared her shoulders. "The only thing I owe you is a dollar for that candy bar you bought me at the police station tonight. Remember? It was right after Niles Winsett told the Pine City Herald reporter that using Carly's Creations was the biggest mistake he'd ever made. And it was right before you locked me in the witness room."

"So pay up."

Carly patted down the front pocket of her Texas Longhorns nightshirt. "Sorry, I seem to have left my billfold in my other pajamas."

His steely eyes never left her face. "Then give me something else instead."

Her heart tripped in her chest. Was this an indecent proposal? Maybe she looked sexier in the tattered football jersey than she thought.

"Information," he continued, before she could even turn him down. "Tell me why you had me pulled off the case."

Carly dug her bare toes into the hallway carpet. "Temporary insolvency?"

"Try again."

"Maybe I just wanted to send you back to the ranch." She refused to let his height or his gun or that sexy scowl on his face intimidate her. Much less tell him the real reason for his pink slip, that she couldn't stand the heat, so she got him out of her kitchen.

"Or maybe you just wanted to get even. That's what this is all about, isn't it, Carly? A little dash of revenge for the big, bad bodyguard."

Her mouth fell open. She closed it again before he could accuse her of some other ridiculous charge, like not flossing. "Revenge? I can't afford that luxury. I'm too busy cleaning up the mess you're making of my life."

He leaned forward, bracing one broad hand on the wall behind her. "You need me. And for more than kitchen detail. You may not value your life, but I do." His intense gaze roamed over her face. "So does the D.A., and the rest of the prosecution team. Don't let your stubborn pride get in the way of what's best for you."

"My stubborn pride?" she echoed in disbelief. "I'm not the one dragging people out of a sound sleep in the middle of the night to discuss job performance." She pushed against the hard wall of his chest. "And for your information, you aren't exactly the best thing that's ever happened to me. Since the moment I met you my life's gone from bad to worse to a complete wreck. I don't want to live without friends and dreams and freedom." She pushed harder, but he didn't budge.

"Don't you get it?" he said between clenched teeth. "They aren't worth anything if you're not around to enjoy them. For crying out loud, your life is at stake! Am I such a controlling monster that you couldn't stand me for a few more days?"

"Yes," she said bluntly.

Jack's eyes narrowed as he grasped her by both

shoulders. "If I can put up with your reckless antics, I think you can put up with a little protective supervision."

His fingers burned through the cotton jersey and into her skin. Well, now at least she knew exactly what he thought of her. Vengeful. Stubborn. Reckless. "What you call protective supervision, I call a slow death by suffocation." Tears stung the back of her eyes. "The point is that I don't have to put up with anything. Not anymore. I can take care of myself, Jack. I always have."

His hands slid down her arms and captured her wrists, pinning them against the wall. "Prove it."

Carly drew in a ragged breath as she resisted the urge to struggle against him. "No, thanks, cowboy. We both know you're bigger than I am. Stronger. Maybe even tougher. But you can't tell me what to do anymore." She moistened her dry lips with the tip of her tongue. "It's over, Jack. I don't want you."

A shiver crawled up her spine at the hunger she saw in his eyes. Without warning, the animosity between them dissolved into a whirlpool of breathless anticipation.

"Prove it," he whispered huskily. And then his mouth came down on hers, hard and hot and irresistible. Releasing her wrists, he threaded his fingers through hers, sliding them slowly up the wall until he held them above her head.

Carly opened herself up to him, not thinking, just feeling. She felt the scrape of his whiskers against her cheek. She felt the silken stroke of his tongue in her mouth. Then the heavy warmth of his body sinking into her softness, trapping her between him and the wall, both rock-hard and unyielding.

She kissed him back with all the fierce frustration that had been building inside her. She tangled her tongue with his in a heated battle that neither could lose, punishing him with her mouth. He took it all and more.

Her pulse pounded as his hands fell away from hers to cup her shoulders. Their previous embraces didn't prepare her for this spiraling ascent into oblivion. Where nothing mattered but tasting and holding him, until she was satisfied.

And they were still standing in the middle of the darn hallway.

She fought for some semblance of control as the turbulence of their passion swirled around her. A shiver rippled through her when she finally tore her mouth away from his.

Gasping for breath, she looked up into those eyes of molten silver and suddenly realized he meant more to her than her friends, her dreams, her freedom. He meant more to her than a one-night stand, especially since Ted lay blocking the path to her bedroom. Swallowing the lump of regret tightening her throat, she said the only thing possible under the circumstances. “Goodbye, Jack.”

9

Bright sunlight filtered through the gauzy curtains of her bedroom window the next morning as Carly awoke from a muddled dream featuring Jack Holden on horseback singing "Save a Horse, Ride a Cowboy." She was confused until she realized the Big & Rich song was playing on the fifth-floor balcony below her open window.

Carly rolled out of her rumpled bed, looked in the mirror, and stifled a scream. The reflection didn't declare her the fairest in the land; it told her she shouldn't have taken that cold shower last night after she left Jack's arms. Her hair had dried naturally and now it stuck out as if she'd been hit with ten thousand volts. In less than three hours she was due to cater the biggest event of her career, Monica Boyle's campaign fundraiser, a sit-down luncheon for one hundred of Pine City's most influential people.

Despite his electrifying kiss, Carly couldn't hold Jack responsible for this latest catastrophe. Or could she? Lunging into her clothes, she thought of all the reasons to blame him. For keeping her awake half the night while she replayed their conversation over and over in her head. For making her stand under that frigid spray of water until the goose bumps pebbling her skin were due to hypothermia instead of the memory of his touch.

A dull throbbing behind her eyes told Carly that she didn't get enough sleep last night. Or she was coming down with something. Maybe Jack gave her the flu as a going away present. As if he could ever outdo his other gifts to her. Like the traffic ticket, the handcuffs, the spilled vichyssoise, the right hook for Mr. Hodges, or the margarita bath for Sidra Collins. The list could go on and on. Just like the list of things she needed to do this morning.

It's just nerves, she told herself, trying to pat down her springy hair with one hand while she applied lipstick with the other. *Pre-catering jitters.* The only thing she'd contracted from Jack was a case of unrequited love. Unfortunately, she doubted even a big bowl of onion gruel could cure her ailing heart.

Carly finished tucking in her blouse, stuck a contact lens in each eye, and then searched under the bed for her shoes. She shoved one black leather flat on and then hopped over to the window while she slung her foot into the other. Holding her breath, she parted the curtains, then her gaze scanned the parking lot. There was no sign of Jack's pickup truck.

He was really gone.

She let the curtain fall as reality set in. He'd finally listened to her. "Goodbye, Jack," she whispered to herself, biting down hard on her lower lip to keep it from trembling.

Telling him goodbye last night had been the hardest thing she'd ever done. The right thing, too, she told herself firmly. Definitely the right thing. Really. Despite the dream. Carly blinked back her tears as she turned on her heel and strode out of the bedroom. Crying over Jack wouldn't put food on the D.A.'s table, or money in her apron pocket.

"Ted," she shouted as she power-walked into the living room. "Time to wake up." Throwing open the drapes, she made a mental list of things to do. *Mix up the dressing for the lobster salad. Soften the gelatin for the jellied tomato madrilene. Alter Jack's catering uniform to fit Ted.*

Her new bodyguard lay stretched out flat on his

wooden board like an insect mounted on a pin. His sparse gray hair was plastered in place across his pink scalp and his faded green shirt gaped between the buttons over his rounded stomach. *Scratch the alterations.* She didn't have enough time or uniform to spare.

“Let's go,” she called, clapping her hands together.

"There's no need for all that racket," he grumbled from his makeshift bed. "I'm awake. That awful music from your downstairs neighbor woke me up an hour ago. What happened to the golden oldies, like Doris Day?" He lifted his peppery brows and crooned, "Que sera, sera. Whatever will be, will be... The future's not ours to see..."

"I already know what my future will be," Carly interjected as she moved toward the kitchen, her mind working furiously to remember everything she needed for the luncheon. *The crepe pan... the pepper mill... at least two cups of whole cloves.* "Incredibly bleak if I don't make it to the community center for the D.A.'s fundraiser on time. We need to leave here in exactly thirty minutes."

"I'm afraid that's not possible, Ms. Weiss."

Carly stifled a groan as she pivoted to face him. "You're not one of those bodyguards who adhere to some rigid set of rules, treat witnesses like common criminals, and never shave, are you?" She didn't wait for a reply, knowing deep down inside there wasn't anyone in the same category as Jack. "Because I'm telling you, Ted, I'm not in the mood for any arguments. And I'll find some way of leaving this place, with or without you." She planted both hands on her hips, trying to look as mean as she sounded.

"I'm one of those bodyguards whose back went out sleeping on this crooked board of yours," he explained, struggling to sit up. "And you're not supposed to go anywhere without me. The D.A. made that perfectly clear to both of us." Carefully dragging his legs over the side of the board, he gripped the back of one chair and hoisted himself to his feet.

Carly wrung her hands together and tried not to panic. "But the mayor's coming today, and several city council members. Did you know the city offers a catering contract for all its official functions? Did you know I could really use a lucrative contract right about now?" She bit her lower lip, fighting a ridiculous urge to cry and spill out all her heartache with her tears. "I can't lose this chance, Ted. Not when I've lost everything else."

He looked away from her and stared down at the hardwood floor. "Sometimes hot water relaxes the back muscles. Help me to the bathroom and I'll try to steam the pain away."

She slung his arm around her neck and half carried him down to the bathroom, desperation or his stale body odor providing her with near superhuman strength. Then she ran back to the kitchen, dumping the crepe pan and a drawerful of utensils into a box before grabbing a handful of cloves out of a bulk bag in her refrigerator.

A brisk knock on the door made her heart skip a beat. Maybe it was Jack. Her hand curled into a fist, pressing the cloves against the tender flesh of her palm. Was he ready to begin round two? Back to tell her how little she valued her life, or how she couldn't live without him? At least until Monday.

Obviously, he didn't know hell hath no fury like a woman running late. She didn't have time to make up more excuses about why she axed him. Maybe she'd do something wild and impulsive instead. Like tell him the truth. That should scare him away. If the sight of her hair didn't do it first.

Carly marched toward the front door, ready to unleash her righteous indignation. This time he better not argue. Better not try to distract her with a kiss. And if he valued his life, better not make one crack about her hair.

This time she'd make him listen to her. If it was the last thing she did.

The chirp of his cell phone alarm woke Jack with a start. He sat up too quickly, hitting his elbow on the steering wheel and grimacing as his legs cramped, stiff from the long night spent in the front seat of his pickup truck. In the light of day, his vigil parked on the street across from the Sagebrush Apartments seemed like the dumbest thing he'd ever done.

All because he saw a man who looked suspiciously like Stanley Jones circling the block when he emerged from the building last night.

Jack flexed his feet in his cowboy boots. His stiff leg muscles seemed insignificant compared to the pain he'd experienced last night when Carly shut the door in his face. He'd stood rigid in the empty hallway, his survival instincts screaming at him to get as far away as possible from Carly. Officially he was off the case. He was a free man, unhindered by duty, responsibility, or kitchen chores. He could return to his new home and go back to building the ranch of his dreams.

But his sense of self-preservation had battled with his conscience. On the one hand, Carly needed protection. On the other hand, Carly needed protection. From him. Before he did something they'd both regret. Like that intimate moment in the apartment hallway.

Jack groaned as he rubbed the corded muscles in the back of his neck. He never lost control like that. Ever. He'd come close, in the Winsett kitchen, for instance. But even then, that small voice of reason in the back of his mind kept him from crossing that line. Kept him from doing something idiotic. Like seducing a woman wearing a Texas Longhorns nightshirt. And little else.

He tipped his head back against the seat, remembering how incredible she'd looked. Long, bare legs. Full, pink lips. Tousled, chestnut hair falling into her eyes.

Just thinking about it made him ache for her. He needed a drink, even if it was too early in the day. He needed a cold shower, even if it wouldn't help one bit.

He needed to get the hell away from Carly.

She didn't want him anyway. His dismissal from the case was proof of that. Fine. Good riddance. So long, sweetheart. From now on Carly Weiss was on her own.

His cell phone rang, but he didn't recognize the number on the screen. "Hello," he answered, his voice rough from sleep.

"Ted Simmons here," came the reply. "I've got a problem."

Jack leaned back against the stiff leather headrest. "I know. Her name is Carly and she's a five-foot-six-inch package of trouble. I wish you a lot of luck, Ted. You're going to need it."

Silence crackled over the line. Then the sound of Ted clearing his throat came through loud and clear. "Well, the thing is, Holden, I need more than luck right now. I heard this witness gave you some trouble, too, so I wanted to ask for your advice."

A reluctant smile curved Jack's lips. Poor old Ted probably got a good dose of Carly's brash, in-your-face attitude this morning. And if that wasn't enough, there was that feisty glow in her indigo eyes, capable of melting away a man's reason faster than butter on a hot skillet. Jack shifted on the leather seat, trying to forget how effectively she'd handled him.

But Ted had forty years of marriage under his belt. Certainly, he didn't need advice on women from a thirty-year-old bachelor. "Just never let your guard down around her. She's smart and darn resourceful. If I were you, I wouldn't let her out of my sight."

A muttered curse came over the line. "It's a little too late for that. She's gone."

Jack straightened up, fully awake now. "What?"

"I said she's gone. Disappeared."

"That's impossible." He'd been watching the apartment building for the last seven hours, give or take the last fifteen minutes when he'd dozed off. The only person he'd seen pass through those doors had been Mrs. Kolinski, walking her poodle. He'd have noticed Carly. Every inch of her was burned into his brain.

"Did you check the hallway?" Jack asked. "Sometimes she sets food out there for stray neighbors."

"No. I haven't checked anywhere. It took me twenty minutes just to crawl to the phone." He paused a beat. "My darned back is out again."

Twenty minutes. Jack's grip tightened around the cold receiver. "How long has it been since you last saw her?"

"About half an hour ago. That's when she helped me into the bathroom."

"Well, her car is still in the parking lot." Jack reached for his cowboy hat. "I'll be right there."

"No, Holden, that's not necessary. It's too much trouble for you to drive all the way across town. I can call Monica," he said, his voice grim, "tell her what happened, and hope she doesn't fire me on the spot." He sighed. "Carly threatened to leave here without me and I just didn't take her seriously."

"Hey, don't worry about it. And it's no trouble,"

Jack replied, glancing up at the faded brick building. “I’m in the neighborhood.”

Two minutes later he walked through the door of Carly’s apartment, telling himself not to assume the worst. Not to overreact. “If anything happens to her, Simmons, I’ll cut you into little pieces and feed you to the birds.”

Ted lay on the hardwood floor beside the television stand, his eyes closed and his complexion pasty white. “Nice to see you again, too, Holden. Hope you didn’t break any traffic laws getting here so fast.”

Jack’s gaze flicked over the living room. His quick assessment of the small apartment showed no signs of a struggle. The locks on the door weren’t broken or even scratched. A large box packed haphazardly with catering supplies sat in the middle of the kitchen floor. None of the potted plants were upturned, no chairs knocked over, not even a pillow out of place on the sofa. Everything looked completely normal.

It scared the hell out of him.

"Seems like she just up and left," Ted said.

Jack shook his head. "Something’s not right here."

He checked the closet and found her catering apron on a hanger and her purse on the wire shelf above it. Fighting back a wave of panic, he let his gaze roam over the living room again, trying to pinpoint what seemed different about her cozy apartment. It just didn't *feel* the same. Empty, somehow. Lifeless. As if Carly took all the warmth and sparkle and vitality with her when she left.

Jack rubbed his eyes with the tips of his fingers. Maybe his sleepless night was making him loopy. Maybe his panic was premature. Maybe she just went out for a walk.

Then he noticed the newspaper folded neatly on the floor by the front door. Reaching over, he picked it up, the front page spilling open to reveal a bold headline reading "Mystery on Mulberry Street?" Beside it was a color photograph of an irate Hubert Hagerty standing over the prone form of Mrs. Niles Winsett. *Maybe she saw this and ran away from home.*

He quickly skimmed the article, a humorous piece detailing how a harmless murder mystery party was crashed by the Pine City police, courtesy of Carly's Creations. The article also featured an interview with District Attorney Monica Boyle assuring the public that no charges were pending against Hubert Hagerty. It concluded with Niles Winsett warning people away from Carly Weiss's catering services.

Talk about an unflattering review.

Guilt and fear knotted inside of him. What if she couldn't accept the possibility of losing her business?

What if the shock of seeing this in print made her do something stupid or careless?

"You've known Carly longer than I have," Ted stated. "Do you think she'd ditch catering this big shindig for the D.A.?"

"No," Jack said briskly. "Carly would never do that." His instincts told him she wouldn't take it lying down, either. She'd fight and finagle and find her way around every obstacle in her path. She'd break every rule in the book to get what she wanted. That reckless tenacity of hers that had driven him crazy for the last four weeks now cheered him considerably. No matter what, Carly Weiss would never give up.

Jack tossed the newspaper on the floor beside Ted.

"Who is Rusty Edwards?" Ted asked, craning his neck to read the subscription label.

"Her creepy next-door neighbor. He gives Carly his newspaper when he's through with it." Jack's gut tightened. "At least he did until four days ago."

"What happened four days ago?"

"Rusty got upset."

Ted sighed. "He must not be upset anymore."

"Maybe." Or maybe not. The hairs prickled on the back of his neck. "Did you call Monica yet? Or the police?"

Ted shook his head, a sheen of perspiration glistening on his brow. "Not yet."

"Well, do it now. Tell them to send a squad car here and one to the community center. If we're lucky, she just went on ahead there without you."

"Where are you going?"

"Someplace I should have checked out a long time ago."

By the time he examined the three locks on Rusty's front door, visions of Carly kidnapped, alone, and in danger had come unbidden to his brain. He finally kicked open the door, focusing all his energy on finding her alive. Only he didn't discover her inside. Or anyone else, for that matter.

What he did see in that apartment left no doubt that Rusty's missing eyebrows weren't the only odd thing about the man. The place looked like an advertisement for Hoarders Anonymous. A dilapidated red velvet love seat huddled in one corner of the room, completely surrounded by endless stacks of books and boxes. Paper littered every inch of the floor.

In the center of one wall was a heart-shaped poster enumerating The Top Ten Traits of True Love. A framed picture of Carly adorned a rickety end table. Another photo of her smiled at him from a wall shelf, and a third hung on the back of the door. All candid shots, taken from a distance. But even

Rusty's amateur efforts managed to capture her fiery spirit.

Jack searched frantically through the rest of the small apartment. He didn't wait for the police or worry that Rusty might freak out about it. He only cared about Carly. And about finding her before it was too late.

His heart beat an erratic tattoo in his chest as he rummaged through drawers and cupboards. Each new piece of evidence he found was like another nail in her coffin. A pad of lavender notepaper. A book of nursery rhymes. An empty gun case.

"Carly, where are you?" he muttered with mounting frustration. He'd already found more than enough clues about Rusty's obsession with his next-door neighbor. Long, rambling, unfinished letters to her. Clipped newspaper articles about the Frey shootings and Carly's vital testimony. Even a lock of her hair. But none telling him where Rusty took her. Or why.

Jack stood in the middle of the chaos and took a deep breath. *Assess the situation, Holden.* He exhaled slowly from his mouth, easing the taut muscles in his neck and shoulders. Carly wasn't here. Which meant Rusty must have taken her somewhere. Forced her somewhere. Jack's gut tightened at the impact of what that could mean. How devoted was Rusty to

Carly? Or his former college professor? And how desperate?

These were questions he didn't have time to ponder. Jack shot out of the apartment and down the hallway to the elevator, determined to find her.

Wishing he had the faintest idea where to look.

"Well, what do you think?" Rusty asked. "Be honest."

"They're gorgeous," Carly replied with excessive enthusiasm. As if she'd dare criticize the handiwork of a man pointing a gun at her. She looked down at the spindly mushrooms growing out of the row of small logs propped against the cinder block wall and tried to think of something nice to say about them. "I had no idea shiitake mushrooms were so... brown."

"It's my surprise for you," he said smugly. "I've been growing them down here in the basement for a really long time. The conditions are perfect. Cool and damp."

She noticed. This dank, abandoned cavern beneath the Sagebrush Apartments reminded her of the old root cellar back home in North Bend. Only this place wasn't filled with comforting jars of homemade preserves and canned beef lining the shelves. No antique butter chum sat unused in the corner.

Instead, discarded wooden crates and plastic tarps lay scattered across the cold cement floor, all coated with a thin layer of grimy dust.

An eerie sense of déjà vu washed over her as Rusty propelled her into the middle of the room. Her brothers used to play war when they were all children, locking her in the cellar as the token prisoner until they reached an armistice agreement or dinner was on the table, whichever came first. She'd never adjusted well to captivity.

A shaft of pale sunlight penetrated the filmy basement windows, illuminating her current prison. A faded quilt hung crookedly from a clothesline, concealing one corner. Cobwebs bridged the rafters in the ceiling. A big black beetle lumbered up the wall. Two baited rattraps lay on the floor.

A shudder ran through her as she forced a phony smile to her lips. Right now, she'd better just worry about that gleam in Rusty's eyes. That I'm-a-raving-lunatic gleam.

He'd hidden it pretty well when he showed up at her apartment this morning with his newspaper. Full of apologies and reserve. His baseball cap planted firmly on his head. A grape juice mustache staining his thin upper lip. And a Smith & Wesson revolver in his hand.

Carly had been so caught up with thoughts of

Jack and the luncheon and her hair that she didn't even notice the gun until he aimed it at her and politely asked if she'd like to go for a stroll with him.

She thought it in her best interests to accept his invitation.

So while Ted crooned "Que Sera, Sera" in the shower, Rusty escorted her to the very bowels of the Sagebrush Apartments building. A crummy place to visit, but she didn't want to die there.

"So, are you excited?" Rusty asked, dusting off an upturned wooden crate for her.

"I'm positively shaking." She sat down and drew her knees up to her chin, wrapping her arms tightly around her legs.

He grinned. "I knew you'd be happy. Fresh shiitake is in high demand and pretty expensive. You told me that once."

"Did I also happen to mention a luncheon I'm due to cater in a couple of hours?" she asked with a quick glance at her watch. Had Ted noticed she was missing yet? Had anyone noticed the trail of cloves she'd dropped along her way? If only Jack was here to inform Rusty that shooting an unarmed woman was against just about everybody's rules.

But Carly was on her own. Responsible for her own second chance at life and love. She'd taken them both for granted lately. Dismissed her feelings for

Jack too easily. *If I survive... when I survive this ordeal with Rusty,* she promised herself, *I'll track Jack Holden down and tell him how I feel, regardless of the consequences.*

"Hey, I've got an idea," she said, diving into her escape plan. "We can serve the mushrooms at my luncheon today. Why don't you get started harvesting while I run up to my place for a big bowl to put them in?"

"I've got everything you need right here." Rusty smiled at her while rubbing his index finger incessantly against the trigger of the gun. Talk about annoying habits.

Still, she didn't want to believe he would really hurt her. Despite his gun. And his road trip from reality. The man cultivated exotic mushrooms for her, after all. He craved her spaetzle. He wore a baseball cap. Surely these things counted for something.

"In fact," he said, "I've got another surprise for you."

Carly didn't know if she could stand any more excitement. "Gee, Rusty, I feel bad because I didn't get you anything. Why don't you let me run out and find you the perfect gift?" *A girlfriend, maybe. Or a straitjacket.*

"You're all I want," he said firmly.

Her heart dropped down to her toes as he raised the gun in the air. But instead of shooting her, he used it to reach out and knock the quilt off the clothesline. It fell into a dusty heap on the floor, revealing a green army cot standing next to the mildewed wall and a worn red velvet armchair sunk unevenly in one corner. A crate served as an end table, stacked with old magazines.

Carly stared in mute disbelief at the tattered furnishings.

"I know it needs a little work," he said with all the enthusiasm of a swampland real estate agent, "but a few pictures... maybe some rugs... will make it nice and cozy. Do you prefer chintz or brocade for the throw pillows?"

The impact of his question blindsided her. "Rusty," she said hoarsely, "you're not planning to... keep me down here, are you?"

He held out his arms. "Surprise."

"This isn't going to work," she insisted as a cold knot formed in her stomach. "The prosecution took my deposition. Professor Frey's trial will proceed whether I'm there to testify or not."

"You've got it all wrong."

Carly began breathing again. "I thought so. This is all some huge misunderstanding. I know you're not the type of man who'd lock me away just to keep me from testifying—"

"Of course not. I want you here on a permanent basis."

He winked at her. "We can make this room our little cozy corner of the world. With your decorating talents and my dehumidifier, everything will be perfect." He furrowed his brow. "Do you think raising shiitake mushrooms will support us until I find a real job?"

Carly unfolded her legs and stood up. "Are you telling me Professor Frey has nothing to do with all of this?"

A blush mantled Rusty's cheeks. "Well, he did encourage me to send you those notes."

She swallowed. "It was you?"

"I made up the rhymes myself and sent the first one to the professor for his approval. He told me sometimes a man has to scare a woman into his arms."

"Why, Rusty?"

He cleared his throat and looked longingly at her. "I wanted to wait until we got all settled in here before I declared my true intentions. But as my favorite professor used to say, love isn't always convenient."

His quoting a hot-blooded killer didn't exactly comfort her. Neither did the knowledge that Rusty penned those notes. The ones that referred to turning a caterer blue and making a date for her with death. She swallowed a scream as he took a step toward her, the gun still aimed at her heart.

"It's true, darling," he continued, obviously interpreting her silence as shocked happiness. "I've loved you from afar. Worshiped you. Now there's nothing standing between us."

Except that loaded weapon in his hands. But why quibble?

"You should have said something sooner, Rusty." *Before you went insane, for instance.* "We could have talked about it."

"I didn't want to talk about it. I wanted to make you need me. Most women run to a man for protection. I thought if you were scared enough, you'd run right into my arms." He blew a fallen cobweb off the barrel of the gun. "And then Jack came along."

Jack. What she wouldn't give for him to come along right about now. Spouting his rules and toting his gun. Providing her with protection from Rusty and any rats lurking in the area.

"He's not really your cousin, is he?" Rusty asked.

"Well... not technically." Carly took a deep breath. "Jack's my bodyguard. He was assigned to protect me after I started receiving your notes. I don't want him to hurt you when he finds us down here," she bluffed. "So maybe you'd better just let me go."

"He's more than your bodyguard," Rusty said, ignoring her suggestion. "I saw you two kissing in the hallway last night."

She swallowed. "I was telling him goodbye."

"That was the longest goodbye kiss I've ever seen." He shook his head wearily. "I think you're lying to me and that's no way to begin our life together. It will only make matters worse."

Worse? How much worse could it get? She thought about the D.A.'s luncheon, the gun aimed at her, the fact Ted couldn't walk without assistance, then told herself not to think anymore. "But it's true. Jack left. For good."

Rusty frowned. "Jack never left. He sat in his pickup truck all night outside the building."

Carly fell back a step. "He did?" Relief coursed through her. Even though she knew Rusty might be mistaken, or more likely, delusional. But she clung to the hope it sparked within her. And the impetus it gave her to escape before Jack came along to say, "I told you so."

"What's really going on between you two?" he asked, his voice heavy with suspicion.

Wonderful. A *jealous, raving lunatic.* Just like Chester Frey. Edging around to the other side of the crate, she replied, "Absolutely nothing."

"I wish I could believe you. But I'm still more

than a little hurt about your fling with Jack. We need to rebuild trust. If you read Professor Frey's book, you'll learn that trust is one of the Top Ten Traits of True Love." He cocked the hammer of his gun. "And trust me, Carly, if you're in love with Jack, I'll be forced to do something we'll both regret."

10

"In love with Jack Holden?" Carly vehemently shook her head. "That's insane." *Whoops.* Nothing like rubbing it in. "I mean the very idea is insane. Everybody thinks so," she added quickly. "Jack and I are like oil and water. Like pork rinds and pâté de foie gras. We just don't go together."

Rusty looked skeptical. "You don't think he's handsome?"

"Well, yeah... I mean, he's all right. In a tall, dashing, cowboy kind of way. He's got broad shoulders," she admitted. "Gorgeous gray eyes and a strong, square chin. If that's what you're looking for in a man."

"And you're not?" he challenged, his fingers tightening nervously around the butt of the gun.

"Puhleeeze!" Carly said, hoping she sounded

convincing. "Tall, dark, and handsome are a dime a dozen. You're a man with intelligence. Style. Stability." *Whoops again.* "A man," she continued quickly, wetting her dry lips with the tip of her tongue, "who can see the potential in a place like this." She encompassed the room with one grand sweep of her hand. "A little candlelight... some bug spray, and we've got a romantic paradise."

"Are you sure?" Rusty regarded her quizzically, a crease furrowing his brow. "The hallway upstairs seemed romantic enough for you last night. Or were you too wrapped up in Jack's kiss to notice the surroundings?"

It was hard to lie to her next-door neighbor, especially since he'd witnessed her meltdown in Jack's arms through his peephole. "You call that a kiss? I shudder just to think about it. All wet and sloppy. Actually," she continued frantically, "it was more like a peck. A friendly peck. A friendly acquaintance peck."

"That friendly acquaintance peck lasted ten minutes." Rusty didn't look persuaded. In fact, he looked downright deranged with jealousy.

Time for Plan B.

"Ahhh," she cried out, putting up one hand to her right eye and bending over at the waist. What it lacked in originality, she made up for with sound effects. A few moans and pained gasps should make him believe she needed emergency assistance. Or at least a reprieve from the interrogation. But Rusty remained unmoved by her apparent agony. He stood motionless in front of her, impatiently tapping one foot on the floor.

"I'm not falling for your fake contact attack routine."

"I'm in a lot of pain, Rusty," she said tightly. "From all the dust. My eyes are really sensitive."

He shook his head in disgust. "I saw you pull this stunt six months ago when you tried to get the cable guy to hook up the premium channels free of charge."

So much for Plan B. She really needed to develop some new material.

"This means you're lying to me," he said furiously. "About everything!"

Carly opened her mouth to protest but the words stuck in her throat when she glimpsed the hollow depths of his eyes. He was way beyond hearing her now. Well past the point of reason.

"All lies," he exclaimed. "Especially about Jack." His breathing grew ragged, making the gun quiver in his outstretched hand. "I won't let him have you, Carly. Not now. Not ever."

The basement door flung open before his cryptic words even registered in her harried brain. She almost jumped out of her shoes at the loud bang of the steel door against the wall.

"Then come and get me, Rusty." Jack's taunting cry echoed across the cavernous room.

The moment Rusty turned his attention and his weapon toward Jack, Carly picked up the wooden crate at her fingertips and threw it at his gun hand. A shot rang out as the gun skittered across the floor.

Jack flew down the stairs in one fluid motion, hurling himself at Rusty. They both landed with a hard thud on the cement. Rusty's scream of surprise was abruptly cut off when Jack drew back his fist and delivered a solid uppercut to the jaw. Rusty's eyes rolled back in his head as he slumped into unconsciousness.

And then it was all over. Carly stood there in stunned silence as overwhelming relief flowed through her, warming the icy blood in her veins. The bizarre events of the morning mingled in her mind, with all the nonsensical chaos of a bad dream. Doris Day. The shiitake mushrooms. Oversleeping on the biggest day of her career. Rusty's armed abduction. Ted's back trouble.

And then Jack. Appearing out of nowhere like a guardian angel in a cowboy hat and faded denim jeans. Rescuing her at the last minute. Protecting her from the danger she'd been too stubborn and proud and blind to see.

The sound of rushing water brought her back to reality. The bullet from Rusty's gun had mortally wounded an old, corroded pipe running up the south wall. A stream of rusty water bled onto the floor, collecting in a pool around the ramshackle love nest Rusty had created for her and drowning the shiitake mushrooms.

Carly's throat tightened as she watched Jack kneel beside Rusty, checking his condition before retrieving the gun from the floor and briskly emptying the bullets from the cylinder. He looked so cool and detached. Every inch the professional. But remote to her somehow. Almost a stranger. She scrambled to say something, anything, to break the unnerving silence between them.

"Did you ever have one of those days," she joked weakly, her voice sounding strained to her ears, "where nothing seemed to go right?"

Jack looked up at her then, his piercing gray eyes bridging the gap between them. He rose, brushing the thick dust off his shirt and jeans. Then he slowly approached her with the measured gait of an animal stalking its prey.

Carly backed up one step before remembering the baited rattraps on the floor behind her. She glanced nervously over her shoulder, and then back at Jack, torn with indecision.

The next instant his hands closed around her shoulders, propelling her away from the light and the rattraps and into the shadows. The smile haunting his solemn face sent a shiver of heated awareness through her.

Without a word he drew a rough finger slowly up the slender column of her neck until he reached her chin and tilted it slightly. Her startled gaze met half-lidded eyes. "So you think I'm a lousy kisser?"

His question throttled the dizzying current of anticipation racing through her. "What?"

One hand slid along her shoulder, curling around the nape of her neck so she couldn't retreat. "*Sloppy*, I believe is the exact word you used," he said roughly, "and *wet*." His fingers flexed as they tangled in her thick curls.

Carly tried to steady her breathing. "You heard that?"

"That and a lot more," he replied. "Your voices carried really well through the door." He urged her closer, without touching his body to hers, intensifying the sultry heat trapped between them.

She wanted him to hold her in his arms. To comfort her. To wipe that smudge of dirt off his nose. Instead, he kept her a hairsbreadth away, berating her with his words while he seduced her with his eyes. The tension coiled so tightly within her suddenly unraveled at his impenetrable control.

"I can't believe you just let me sweat it out down here with a crazed, aspiring killer so you could eavesdrop at the door," she said. "So much for your protection! What exactly were you waiting for? An engraved invitation from Rusty?" She ignored the brilliant warning in his eyes. "Or a rave review from me for your performance in the hallway last night?"

"Maybe I just needed a little time to recover from the revelation that your contact attack my first day on the job was just a stunt." His voice sounded deep and dark and dangerous. "A ploy obviously designed to manipulate me into catering for you."

"You needed time?" she scoffed, the erratic beat of her heart having nothing to do with fear for her physical safety. "The man held me at gunpoint long enough for you to grow a beard." She looked pointedly at the thick black stubble on his face. "Maybe you spent some of that time wondering if a woman as vengeful... as reckless..." She slung back each dart he'd thrown at her last night. "...as stubborn as I am, deserved to be rescued. Making me pay the consequences for breaking every one of your precious rules."

Carly drew in a deep, shaky breath. Her nerves

were stretched taut. "Just exactly how long did you linger out there?"

Jack lifted his hand to tenderly brush a wayward curl off her cheek. "Long enough to realize how brave you are. And gutsy. And smart. Long enough to know I can't live without you."

His unexpected admission drained every ounce of frustrated indignation out of her. It seemed too preposterous on top of everything else. Too fantastic. "Did you hit your head on the cement when you tackled Rusty?"

"No. But I hit Rusty harder than necessary." He gently tipped her head back to rain soft, hungry kisses on her nose and cheeks. "It felt wonderful. Almost as wonderful as you."

A tiny gasp escaped Carly's lips as he pulled her into his arms. "I can't believe I almost lost you," he murmured into her curls. "If it wasn't for that trail of cloves, I'd be tearing Pine City apart brick by brick right now looking for you."

He held her tightly against him, as if he never intended to let her go. His lips nuzzled the hollow behind her ear before tenderly capturing the soft lobe with his teeth.

"I love you, Jack," she whispered against his unshaven cheek. Her hands curled around his thick forearms to keep him from escaping at her confession. "Maybe it is insane, but I love you with all my heart. Even if we are complete opposites."

"Pork rinds and pâté de foie gras?" He abandoned her ear to ply her with a teasing smile—one full of love and relief and promise.

"Exactly." Carly traced the outline of his smile with her fingertip. "But I'm sure we can adapt. You already know I have strong objections about following orders and I have incontrovertible evidence that you're a complete disaster in my kitchen. Not that it matters much anymore. The D.A. will probably want to throw the book at me for missing her luncheon. She'll never hire me again and certainly won't recommend my services to any of her powerful cronies. I'll be lucky if she doesn't sue me for breach of contract..."

He placed a quieting finger against her lips. "Carly."

"Yes, Jack?"

"Shut up and kiss me," he whispered, lowering his mouth to hers.

His mouth was warm and heavy and seductively demanding against her own. He kissed her with barely leashed desire that set fire to her senses. Carly felt her whole body soften with need and love for him. In that moment, she knew the exquisite power of what it meant to feel both safe and free.

"I want to be alone with you," he said hoarsely, his arms tightening around her. "But we're still standing in the middle of this darn cellar."

"I know," she murmured against his mouth. "We've got to stop meeting like this."

Jack groaned softly as he set her away from him. "I've got a solution. But it means following one last order." He threaded his fingers through hers and brought one hand to his lips, turning it over to tenderly kiss her open palm. "And obeying it without question."

The sensation of his lips against her skin made it difficult to think. Or breathe. "That's asking a lot of me."

"More than you realize." He looked deeply into her eyes. "Marry me, Carly. I've got a big kitchen in my new house and plenty of room on the ranch to grow all the garden produce you need for your catering business." He pulled her closer to him. "But most of all, you're the only woman I know who could ever make it feel like home."

She smiled and sank into him, winding her arms around his neck. "Yes, Jack, I'll marry you."

After a long, lingering kiss that left them both gasping for air, he murmured, "I could get used to this."

She laughed from sheer joy as her fingers traveled

over the muscular terrain of his broad shoulders. “Get used to what? My unquestioning obedience or passion in unusual places?"

“You in my arms,” he replied, drawing her closer to show her just what he meant.

“Jack,” she said breathlessly, after another formidable demonstration of his affection. “Do you know what this means? I can be a farm-to-table caterer. And I can try out all my new recipes on you. Just think of all the opportunities there!”

“Believe me, I am,” he said huskily, dropping a string of heated kisses down her throat to her shoulder. “Unlimited opportunities. I plan to take advantage of every single one.”

A dreamy sigh escaped her lips. “With that kind of devoted enthusiasm, we’ll be creating more than fine cuisine.” She arched an inquisitive brow. “Are you up to the job, Jack Holden?”

He pressed her close. “I can’t wait to show you.”

Before he could elaborate, Ted Simmons noisily lumbered down the concrete stairs, supported on either side by a uniformed police officer.

Carly almost laughed aloud at the blush on Jack’s cheeks as he circled his arms protectively around her waist and drew her out of the shadows.

“About time you showed up,” Jack said without

enthusiasm. "We've got a man here who needs medical assistance and a lot of jail time."

Ted groaned and placed one hand against his lower back as he descended down the last step. "We would've been here sooner, but we got stuck in that darn elevator." His disbelieving gaze took in the tattered furnishings, the smashed wooden crate next to Rusty's inert body, and the water gushing from the busted iron pipe. "What in the hell happened down here?"

Carly grinned up at him. "Jack and I just got engaged."

EPILOGUE

Jack knew marriage to Carly wouldn't be boring. But he assumed he'd make it through the engagement in one piece. At least until her three big brothers strolled into the Wildcat Tavern and looked around with menacing expressions. He recognized them from a video chat with her family and the photos Carly had shown him of her family.

"Looks like my future brothers-in-law just walked in," Jack said, picking up his beer mug and pointing them out to Hank, Trace, and Cade. The four Holden brothers had just ordered their nachos and pizza.

"I thought Carly was coming with them," Trace said, leaning back in his chair and folding his arms across his chest.

"She was, but she must have gotten held up at her

catering gig." Jack waved a hand in the air to get their attention. "Hey, fellas, over here."

The three Weiss brothers exchanged glances with each other, then lumbered toward the table.

"They don't exactly look happy to see you," Cade observed with an amused smile.

Jack rose to his feet. "No, they don't."

"Maybe they heard how you handcuffed their sister," Hank said with a grin. "And want a little payback."

Jack sighed, thinking his big brother might be right. But he had no regrets. Carly was safe now. A month after the trial, Professor Chester Frey was locked away in prison for the rest of his life, thanks to Carly's testimony. The jury had returned with a guilty verdict in record time. And Rusty was in a mental facility getting the help he sorely needed.

"Which one of you is Jack?" the tallest of the Weiss brothers asked when they reached the table.

"I'm right here," Jack said, holding out his hand. "You must be Robby."

Robby folded his arms across his chest. "Why don't we take this outside, Jack? We've got a few things to say to you."

Cade rose to his feet, along with Hank and Trace. "I'm thinking maybe we'll join y'all."

"No," Jack said to his brothers, determined to

handle this alone. "You boys just stay here and order another round. We won't be long."

Trace shrugged. "Okay, have fun," he called out as Jack followed the Weiss brothers to the back door of the tavern.

Once they were outside, Robby closed the door behind them, and then all three Weiss brothers faced Jack with the cool detachment of a firing squad.

“Look, Holden,” growled the bear of a man called Robby, the oldest of the Weiss bunch. “We'll put it to you bluntly. Marriage to our sister is not for the faint-hearted.”

Brad and Bret sidled up next to their brother, their bulging biceps rubbing against each other. “That's right,” chimed Brad. “We don't need or want a coward in our family.”

“Especially a total stranger who plans to keep our baby sister from coming home to North Bend,” Bret added. The three of them formed an impenetrable barricade in front of the door.

Jack stifled a sigh of irritation. Their timing couldn't be worse. Soon, Carly would arrive at the tavern for their engagement celebration, along with Grandma Hattie and the rest of his family. A party he didn't intend to miss. Although this confrontation didn't surprise him.

Ever since he and Carly had joined her family on a

video chat to announce their engagement, Jack had gotten the feeling that her brothers didn't approve. They'd made it pretty clear that they didn't trust their sister's fiancé any farther than they could throw him. Which judging by their beefy size, was a considerable distance.

"I only want to make Carly happy," Jack said evenly.

"That's all we want, too," Robby said. "We're just not convinced you're the man to do it."

Jack's gaze roamed over his future brothers-in-law, assessing the situation. Three against one. He drew himself up for battle. Carly might not appreciate a family brawl before the party, but he had no intention of letting these three bully him out of her life. Not after everything he'd been through to get here.

"I suppose I need to prove it to you," he said, taking a step closer to them.

"Good idea," Bret replied, removing his denim jacket and draping it over an empty beer keg. "This will give us a chance to see just what you're made of, Holden."

Jack rolled up his sleeves, then waited for his opponent to declare himself ready. He had to give the Weiss boys credit; they obviously intended to take him on one at a time. At least they fought fair.

"See this?" Bret asked, walking up to Jack with his fist in the air.

Jack stood with his feet planted wide apart and arms at his sides. He'd let good old Bret throw the first punch for the sake of family harmony. Jack almost couldn't blame them for wanting to protect someone as precious as Carly.

Bret pointed to a pale scar laced across his forearm. "I got this when Carly decided to float down Bannock Creek in a barrel for her tenth birthday. When I went after her, I sliced it open from my elbow to my wrist on an old rusty car fender submerged underwater. Ten stitches."

"Show him your knee," Brad prompted.

Bret pulled up his pant leg to display a shiny white patch of skin in the middle of a hairy shin. "This happened when she talked me into exploring an abandoned cave one summer afternoon when she was eleven. I tripped over an old miner's shovel and landed on the campfire she built to keep all the bats away." He massaged the bare skin with his fingertips. "Skin graft."

"That's nothing," scoffed Robby, bending over and parting the thinning chestnut hair on his head. "You see this bump? Carly whacked me with a broom handle when I snuck into the house one night after curfew. She heard a noise and thought I was a burglar."

"She forgot to put on her glasses," supplied Bret.

"She could still see well enough to give me a concussion." Robby rubbed the old wound with tender fingers. "I had double vision for three months after that."

"What about the time she ran up that willow tree?" Brad offered.

A reminiscent smile curved Jack's lips. "I heard about that little escapade."

Robby snorted. "Did she tell you she took pictures of the three of us being rescued by the fire department, then sold them to the *North Bend Gazette* for ten dollars apiece?"

"She wanted to buy a cookbook," Brad informed him.

Bret placed a hand over his stomach. "Which reminds me of the time she baked that quiche."

"Using those wild roots she picked by Wilkin's Pond," Robby added, with one hand over his own stomach.

"Food poisoning," Brad stated, his complexion turning a pale green at the memory. "All three of us."

"In the North Bend Community Hospital," Bret said.

"Getting our stomachs pumped," Robby added.

"During North Bend High School's only appearance in the state football playoffs," Brad finished forlornly. "The three of us made up most of the offensive line on the team. They dedicated the game ball to us."

"Our team lost sixty-two to three," Robby said with a mournful sigh.

Jack rolled his sleeves back down and buttoned his cuffs. Marriage into the Weiss family might not be so bad after all. They could all get together at Thanksgiving and Christmas and compare battle scars.

"So, we're giving you fair warning, Holden," Bret said. "You marry Carly and we expect you to stay by her side for better or for worse."

"And there will be plenty of worse," Brad warned. "So you better think long and hard before you make any vows you don't intend to keep."

"Because despite how many bones we've broken on account of our little sister," Robby said, "we won't let any man break her heart."

Jack straightened the collar of his shirt and then faced them squarely. How could he verbalize the endless depth of his love for her? The pride he felt when her testimony sealed the case against Frey. The intimacy they shared. The joy she brought to his life. Even when she dragged him to the grand opening of

Pine City's newest pancake house to celebrate the reconciliation of Alma and a clean and sober Stanley. He'd never had so much fun with maple syrup before.

How did he explain that Carly simply made his life complete?

"I can't predict the future," he began. "But I know I love Carly more than my life. So we'll face it together. Every unpredictable, bumpy step of the way."

"Is that all?" asked Robby.

Jack surveyed the three men with a critical eye. Each bore at least one scar that proved how much they loved the woman he planned to marry. They wanted proof that he could handle whatever she dished out to him.

"I've received survival training at Quantico."

They looked completely unimpressed.

"I've got an exceptionally high tolerance to pain."

Bret raised a skeptical brow.

"I've lived with Carly and still want to marry her."

"What do you mean, you *lived* with her?" growled Robby. Jack suddenly realized Carly hadn't told her family about all the events in Pine City. "I was her bodyguard."

Bret laughed out loud. "That's a good one, Holden."

"It's the truth."

"You actually stayed with Carly? In the same apartment?" Brad asked in disbelief.

"For the four longest, most frustrating, wackiest weeks of my life," Jack replied with a grin.

"He's still walking, too," Bret said. "Gee, Robby, maybe he's the man for Carly after all."

"Maybe he is," Robby said begrudgingly. Then he slapped Jack on the back. "Welcome to the family, Holden. Now let's see how well you can party."

Jack followed them back into the tavern where they joined the rest of the Holden clan. A few minutes later, he saw his feisty, beautiful fiancée walk through the front entrance and head for their table. He met her halfway.

Just as he intended to do for the rest of their lives.

Dear Reader,

Thank you so much for reading *Cowboy Bodyguard.* If you enjoyed Jack and Carly's story, we would so appreciate a review. You have no idea how much it means to us!

Please look out for the final book in the Cowboy Confidential series, *Cowboy Daddy,* due out in 2022.

If you'd like to keep up with our latest releases,

you can sign up for Lori's newsletter @ https://loriwilde.com/subscribe/

Or follow Lori on Bookbub. https://www.bookbub.com/profile/lori-wilde

To check out other books, you can visit us on the web @ www.loriwilde.com.

Much love and light!

—Lori & Kristin

ALSO BY LORI WILDE AND KRISTIN ECKHARDT

COWBOY CONFIDENTIAL

Cowboy Cop

Cowboy Protector

Cowboy Bounty Hunter

Cowboy Bodyguard

Cowboy Daddy

ABOUT THE AUTHOR

Kristin Eckhardt is the author of 49 novels with over two million copies sold worldwide. She is a two-time RITA award winner who loves writing romantic fiction. Her debut novel was made into a television movie called Recipe for Revenge. After earning a degree in Animal Science, Kristin and her husband raised three children on a farm on the Nebraska prairie. Along with writing, she enjoys baking, sewing, and spending time with family and friends.

Lori Wilde is the New York Times, USA Today and Publishers' Weekly bestselling author of 96 works of fiction. She's a three time Romance Writers' of America RITA finalist and has four times been nominated for Romantic Times Readers' Choice Award. She has won numerous other awards as well.

Her books have been translated into 26 languages, with more than four million copies of her books sold worldwide.

Her breakout novel, *The First Love Cookie Club*, has been optioned for a TV movie. And her *Wedding*

Veil Wishes series has inspired three movies currently being filmed by Hallmark.

Lori is a registered nurse with a BSN from Texas Christian University. She holds a certificate in forensics, and is also a certified yoga instructor.

A fifth generation Texan, Lori lives with her husband, Bill, in the Cutting Horse Capital of the World.

SNEAK PEEK OF LORI WILDE'S SECOND CHANCE CHRISTMAS

Chapter One—The Girl

What on earth was she going to do?

It was three days before Christmas and she had no money, no food and no place to stay. Every measly thing she owned was tucked inside the battered backpack weighing heavy on her shoulders.

Shivering in her in her thin jacket, not nearly warm enough for the winter storm rolling through North Central Texas, the teen tightened her grip on the tiny bundle in her arms.

Some dude she barely knew had said she could couch surf with him for a couple of days, but the guy had been adamant. *No brats allowed.*

Panic rose in her throat, swelling and bubbling

like the sourdough starter Grammy fed on her kitchen counter. No, not anymore. Grammy and her sourdough were gone forever, and she was all on her own.

A gust of wind blowing off Lake Twilight, shook the tinsel garlands strung from quaint lantern lamp-posts. Gaily colored lights flickered through the thickening darkness like fickle beacons. On-off. On-off. Her teeth chattered, braces clicking together. Her bare knee, poking from the hole in her jeans, turned as numb as her nose.

For the past three hours, she'd ringed the entire town square, entering boutiques and restaurants to get in out of the cold, leaving when shop owners started giving her dirty looks.

In one restaurant, with hunger gnawing a hole in her stomach, she'd pretended to need to use the restroom, then slipped into the dining area targeting an un-bussed table and flitching leftovers.

It wasn't stealing, she'd told herself. The food was getting thrown out.

Then she saw a ten-dollar bill on the next table and her heart leaped. *That was stealing.* She inched over, reached for the ten, and had it in her fingers when one of the servers caught her.

"Put that back!"

She dropped the ten. "I wasn't—"

"You were."

"I—"

"Get out. Now!"

Ducking her head, she moved toward the door. As she passed, the server whispered "you're disgusting" with a curled lip. Then the woman's gaze landed on the baby tucked up underneath her jacket and the curl had become a full-on snarl. "For shame! What kind of mother are you?"

That was a knife through her heart. She was a horrible mother. She knew it. The baby would be much better off without her.

"Get out." the server said. "before I call the cops."

She'd slunk away, slipping into the shop next door, but they were closing up and she'd had to move on. Now, the only place open was Fruit of the Vine, a storefront for a local winery. It would be six years before she was old enough to legally go inside.

Fighting back tears, she hitched the baby to her shoulder. He'd been really quiet today, almost as if he understood the trouble that they were in.

"Good boy," she cooed to him, making sure the little knitted cap rested securely on his head. "You're such a good boy and Mommy loves you so much."

Earlier, the town square had been packed with shoppers, but now the streets were nearly empty. The vendors on the courthouse lawn had battened down their kiosks and the Santa Land display was shutting earlier. From the outdoor speakers mounted on the courthouse, Christmas music played. "It's the Most Wonderful Time of the Year."

She bit her bottom lip, so dry and cracked from the cold wind that it hurt. The hot tears she'd been battling spilled over the rim of her lower lids and trickled down her face.

Hopeless.

Everything was hopeless.

She fisted her hands against the baby's back. If only she didn't have him. Closing her eyes, she groaned. That server was right. She was a horrible, horrible mother. She sucked in a deep breath of cold air and opened her eyes.

A white church spire topped with a cross rose up behind the buildings on the square. Grammy used to take her to church every Sunday. Her grandmother liked to sit on the front row, to be "closer to God."

"Sorry, Grammy," she whispered, her heart plunging into her throat. "Right now I'm as far away from God as I can get."

She'd tried praying, oh yes, she had, but God must have turned his back on her, because she'd had no answers and her problems kept stacking up like cord wood.

Maybe the church spire is an answer.

She'd seen a program on TV once that said churches were considered "safe havens." A place to anonymously leave your baby if you couldn't take care of it. The only catch was that there had to be someone around to find the baby or it would be considered child endangerment. Or so the program had said. That is if she was remembering correctly.

Trembling now, at her wits end, she walked toward the white steeple sticking up out of the darkness, no real plan in her head. The wind was in her face and she ducked her head to shield the baby, cradling him against her chest. She could feel his little heart beating against hers.

She walked a block, turned right, then left, another block and there it was, the First Presbyterian Church of Twilight.

The building looked old, like it had been built back in the cowboy days, but it had a fresh coat of paint and it was decked in holiday decorations that included an elaborate nativity scene on the front lawn, complete with live animals milling around in a wooden corral.

Her gaze fell on the straw bed where the Baby Jesus lay nestled, surrounded by life-sized plastic figurines of Mary, Joseph, the three wise men and shepherds. The bed looked really warm and it was located underneath a shelter out of the wind.

Should she? Could she?

Her heart was pounding a million beats a second and her face was so cold she could scarcely breathe. But how could she leave him when there was no around to find him? Despair knocked against her chest. A hollow numb feeling that her bewildered and frightened.

She chewed a ragged fingernail, gnawing off the chipped polish—Cotton Candy Daydreams. Last year, Grammy had put the polish in her Christmas stocking. This year there would be no stocking, no presents, nothing. Fresh tears welled in her eyes, stinging her cheeks.

"I'm not leaving you for good," she mumbled, trying to convince herself it was true. "Just until I can find a safe place for us to stay."

The sound of voices sent her shrinking into the shadows, hiding in the thick shrubbery surrounding the church. She crouched, grateful that the baby was sleeping. He was such a good boy. He deserved a good mom. A mom who knew how to love him the right way. He deserved a good dad and a happy home. All things she couldn't give him.

Salty tears filled her mouth, as her heart broke right in two.

The voices grew louder and from around the

opposite side of the church, closest to where the animals were penned, two people appeared.

It was a tall guy who looked to be the age of her dad when she'd last heard from him. Kinda old. Thirtyish. The woman was younger and not much taller than she was. Five-four maybe. The woman wore black motorcycle boots, thick black leggings, a short red plaid skirt and cute white ski jacket. Dope outfit. She had wicked fashion sense.

"You should have worn gloves," the man said to her. "You're hands are turning red."

"I didn't know it was going to get this cold." The woman tucked her hands into her jacket pockets. "It'll be fine."

The man stopped underneath the security lamp that cast a soft glow over the nativity scene, took off his own gloves and tucked them under his arm pit. "Give me one of your hands."

"What?" The woman drew back. "Why?"

"C'mon, Tink." The man grinned. "Just do it."

Narrowing her eyes, the woman slowly took a hands from her pocket and held them out to him.

Gently, he took one of her hand and rubbed it vigorously between both of his hands. Then he repeated the process with her other hand.

Aww, that was so sweet. She wished she had a nice boyfriend who would warm her hands up for her.

Feeling jealous, she pressed her back against the side of the building watching the couple tease each other as they went about turning off the inflatable Christmas decorations on the opposite side of the lawn. They were so nice to each other. Smiling and joking. No yelling or hitting. She could tell they really liked each other. She liked them too.

Safe haven.

The words popped into her head. People were here now. The church was officially a safe haven.

The baby whimpered; a soft little mewl.

If she was going to do this, now was the time while the couple was still here, and their attention was on the other side of the church from where she crouched.

But first, she needed to write a note explaining that she'd be back for him as soon as she could. Quietly, she twisted around, grateful for the relentless wind because it muffled her sounds, she fished a sharpie from her backpack. Then realized she didn't have any paper.

How could she leave a note with no paper? She dug in the backpack, desperate for something to write on and her hand hit a diaper.

His last diaper.

The one she'd been saving for when he did number two.

In the darkness, she wrote a heartfelt note on the diaper, tucked it inside the blanket with him, and as the couple's backs were turned, she crept to the manger, and replaced the plastic Baby Jesus with her son.

Made in the USA
Coppell, TX
12 October 2022